Ramsgate Calling

Sally Forrester

Saint Petersburg, Florida

Print ISBN: 978-1-64718-850-4
Epub ISBN: 978-1-64718-851-1
Mobi ISBN: 978-1-64718-852-8

Published by BookLocker.com, Inc., St. Petersburg, Florida.

Printed on acid-free paper.

BookLocker.com, Inc.
2020

First Edition

Disclaimer

This book may offer health information, but this information is designed for educational, and entertainment purposes only. The content does not and is not intended to convey medical advice and does not constitute the practice of medicine. You should not rely on this information as a substitute for, nor does it replace, professional medical advice, diagnosis, or treatment. The author and publisher are not responsible for any actions taken based on information within.

Sally with Mary's Jack Russell terrier, Winston

The painting of poppies on the front cover and the line drawings in this book are by the author.

Dedication

For my auntie Lillian with much love and to the very fond memory of Anthony James Reid (16th September 1985 – 25th January 2020.)

Anthony with Kate, Sophia and Jack

About the author

Sally's parents, Pat and Evelyn Forrester, came to the Isle of Thanet in the late 1940s on their honeymoon; they loved it so much that they stayed. Sally was born and grew up in the little holiday town of Margate, and first left when she finished St. George's School to attend teacher-training college. Although she moved to the USA with her husband and two sons in 1994 Sally always returns to the area, usually for several months during the summertime, and to celebrate Christmas with relatives. Over the years she has witnessed the area decline and rise once again in fortune. Margate and the surrounding Thanet area are in her blood and hold a special place in her heart. This is Sally's second novel; she has worked as a teacher, artist and in the holistic health field. Her passion is to help people get well and enjoy life. Sally weaves her extensive knowledge and experience of healing with herbs, homoeopathy and flower remedies into this second book and draws her inspiration from the many suffering people who, over the years, have come to tell their story.

The upturn in fortunes of old town Margate inspired Sally to set her books in the Madam Popoff Vintage Emporium. Yes, it is a real shop and a delightful place but the Madam Popoff of Sally's first book *Last Train to Margate* is purely a work of fiction, as are the things that cross Madam's threshold, the characters, and their stories. Now Sally continues the story in the nearby town of Ramsgate where the fictitious Madam

Popoff opens up a second vintage emporium. For her second novel Sally draws upon the colourful history of Ramsgate and the surrounding area. Although this too is a work of fiction some of the people and events are factual, this becomes clear as the reader enjoys the book.

Sally met Mary and her little dog, Winston, at Ship Shape Café in Ramsgate and they too are real. Winston loves his daily sausage dished out by the doting café staff. When Sally is at home in the USA she enjoys sailing her yacht around the coastal waters of Florida and consulting with the many families who seek out her help.

If the reader would like to know more about the real Madam Popoff Vintage in Margate Old Town please review their web site: www.madampopoff.com

Chapter 1

It was early September and Poppy had returned from her European adventure, refreshed and very eager to begin another journey of discovery with Madam Popoff. She was cycling along the prom with Jack the Lad who was snuggled down into the large wicker basket attached to the handlebars. Poppy was thinking about the value of things. Her hiking holiday in the Alps had offered her plenty of thinking time and she had carefully reflected upon all that happened since she had become gainfully employed at the Madam Popoff Vintage Emporium in Margate old town.

The word *value* seemed very important right now. So many people *value* possessions and set great store upon what they own. Madam Popoff had taught Poppy the *value of rightful ownership*. Once again she was reminded of Madam's words, "Poppy dear, there are some things in life that we want, that we can well afford, but actually they do not belong to us and they won't be happy with us."

Poppy had begun to live her life in a much more mindful way. She was thinking before she spoke. She was beginning to use all of her senses and she had learnt to let go of things that really no longer had a place in her life. At long last she had found the energy and the inspiration to sort through the large number of things that she had put into a London storage unit before she had taken that *Last Train to Margate* back in the summer of 2017.

"Clearing out the closets" left room for the new things. She looked forward to meeting new people, having new adventures, and gaining new insights. Poppy understood and comprehended the *value* of loved ones, positive character traits such as courage, strength, conviction, patience and reverence for everything. Her experience with the things that had crossed the threshold of Madam's shop had taught her many important life lessons.

During her European holiday Madam had found a new place for Poppy, a tiny little store in the heart of the old town Ramsgate, and a stone's throw from the harbour and Ship Shape Café. Apparently it had required a great deal of loving care. The premises were old but Madam conjured up a number of willing helpers who all put their skills to good use. Over the years Madam had helped a lot of local people in one way or another and now they were eager to repay. John and his son, Jimmy, were carpenters. Dick and his wife, Gloria, were painters and decorators and Eric was a plumber. When Madam asked they all came to assist and within six weeks the little store sparkled. Loving hands replaced rotten window frames and floorboards. New white, black and gold paint adorned the exterior and the interior was painted a subtle shade of dove grey and delicate pink. Ollie, the harpist, asked an artist friend to come and paint a large mural on one of the interior walls of poppies blowing in the wind. A few costume rails lined the other wall and down the centre heavy old oak dressers from Scott's Emporium served as one very large countertop. It was the perfect place to display costume jewellery, shoes, hats, gloves and other paraphernalia. The drawers were ideal for general storage.

The back room, always an important place in Madam Popoff's world, was tiny. There was just enough room for a sink unit, electric teakettle and cupboard above to house an eclectic mix of fine porcelain china cups, saucers, teapots and cake plates. The cupboard also accommodated a couple of cake tins for the chocolate cake, a most important item. Madam always set great store upon the chocolate and would often say, "It brings people together and helps to mend the broken hearts." Poppy was reminded of Madam's purpose and great mission in life, "To dress and mend the broken pieces, that's what we do here, Poppy." A broom cupboard and a tiny toilet completed the picture and a large costume mirror divided the back room from the shop floor.

Since the back room was so small Madam had set two small but very comfortable armchairs on a brightly patterned blue rug at the back of the store. A tiny oak coffee table divided the two and a little velvet cushion bed had been set out on the rug for Jack the Lad. Poppy knew that this was the place where those needing the most help would find solace. She knew that Madam would expect her to offer her hands, her time and her full attention. Poppy was expected to offer wise counsel because Madam had decided that her student, at long last, was ready.

Poppy knew deep in her heart that she was indeed ready and Ramsgate was calling. She clutched her little tattered booklet, *The Twelve Healers* written by Dr. Edward Bach. This was her greatest treasure. It was the thing that offered the most *value* in Poppy's life, and it was priceless. Poppy knew that Madam and Edward Bach were encouraging her to don the mantle of a healer. Madam decided that, *The Madam Popoff and Poppy Vintage Emporium* would open on Fridays and over the weekend. Poppy would have Monday and Tuesday to herself and Wednesday and Thursday would be spent back at *The Mother Ship* in old town Margate.

The refuge had been prepared, the healer was ready and Madam announced that there would be a grand opening ceremony and party in the afternoon on Monday September 24th because it was deemed to be a very auspicious day. Poppy later discovered that it was the birthday of Edward Bach. "Gosh Madam really does know everything!" She exclaimed to Jack The Lad as she continued to cycle along the prom in the bright September sunshine.

Chapter 2

Poppy was extremely busy leading up to the grand opening on September 24th. Certainly there was a great deal to sort out. Madam asked Ollie and Cedric to rent a truck from B&Q to transport a large amount of merchandise; bags and boxes to stock the new venue and Poppy busied herself with the pricing and arranging. There were two nice picture windows framing the shop door and she carefully arranged an eye-catching display of party dresses and other items together with party hats and streamers to entice the curious and adventurous to cross the threshold. The shop was small; there was no room for tables and chairs to accommodate a tea party but Isadora from the Margate shop came up with a brilliant idea. There was plenty of pavement outside the shop front so it was decided that Madam would write a letter to the local council asking for permission to set out tables and chairs just for the party on September 24th and much to everyone's delight permission was granted. There was always the possibility of rain but Madam insisted that they all thought about sunshine, blue skies and joy and with so many positive thoughts the angels would surely listen. Well, listen they did, and it was a wonderful afternoon. Aunt Flora read the tealeaves, Isadora and her sister baked a large batch of homemade cakes, Ollie brought his harp and Cedric played the violin. A considerable sum of money was collected in aid of the Ramsgate Lifeboat. Business was brisk and Poppy sold a number of items. The local people were excited and there was much enthusiasm for this vintage emporium. After all it appealed to all the bright young folk who came down from London, frequented the town, and had plenty of extra cash to spend.

Chapter 3

It was a Sunday morning in mid-October. Poppy was settling nicely into her new role as manageress of *The Madam Popoff and Poppy Vintage Emporium.* Things were beginning to slow down, the curious and the adventurous had come, explored and left, the town's visitors were now dwindling as autumn had brought with it a cold snap. Jack the Lad still enjoyed his cycle rides along the cliff top to Ship Shape Cafe where Winston and the sausages were always waiting to greet his arrival. Cycling up into old town Ramsgate was definitely a new experience. Usually Poppy had routinely taken him back to Lookout Retreat before continuing her cycle ride into Margate. Jack the Lad was curious at first; there were lots of nooks and crannies to explore in the old building. Eventually he settled into a routine of quiet slumber upon the new velvety cushion that had been provided for his convenience and exclusive use. He enjoyed the loving attention of old ladies and children who crossed the threshold and wanted to pat his silky coat and tickle behind his ears.

Today, Poppy wheeled Dora, her trusty old bicycle, around to the rear of the store and chain-locked her to an adjoining lamppost. Then she carefully dragged a heavy wooden trunk across the threshold. A passer-by must have seen the discreet notice that she had recently placed in one of the large picture windows:

We always welcome vintage donations, when you spring clean please do think of us. Thank you!

The trunk was old and it had a peculiar smell. "It must have been shut away in an attic or a basement for a very long time," she muttered to Jack the Lad. Poppy made herself a cup of coffee and settled into one of the comfortable armchairs at the rear of the store. It was still early. She wasn't expected to open up for a few hours so there would be plenty of time to sift through the contents. Much to her delight, the trunk contained a number of beautiful dresses from the Victorian era. They had been carefully folded and on top of the pile lay a few pairs of ladies gloves and a vintage straw hat decorated with long flowing silk ribbons in shades of pale pink and lemon. This was a major find; Poppy knew that Madam would be pleased. Amongst the pile of carefully folded dresses Poppy discovered a very odd piece of clothing. Following careful examination she decided that it must be a wealthy gentleman's smoking jacket. The material was silk, a deep shade of red and the jacket was decorated with very fine embroidery. Two dragons, one in gold thread and the other one in black, faced each other either side of the front opening. Their long tails curled around and came together at the centre of the back seam. It really was exquisite. Poppy held it up to her nose she could still discern the pungent smell of pipe tobacco. She finished her coffee and relaxed back into the plump cushions of her chair. The jacket lay on her lap, her long fingers rested on the dragon's heads and she drifted off, back to another time.

It was early June in 1868 and Bessie was busy in her kitchen, there was always plenty to do. The Household had recently moved to Ramsgate for the summer season. Local land developers Messes Sankey, Barnet, Hodgson and Pugin had purchased a plot of land on Ramsgate's east cliff and built 8 terraced houses in the popular gothic style. They were substantial properties with four floors and a basement. Each house had a private entrance and they were all marketed as exclusive villas to be let for several weeks at a time to wealthy visitors coming to Ramsgate.

Bessie's employer, Lord Frederick, decided that it would do his sick wife, Lady Louise, the world of good to take in the sea air and reside in Ramsgate for the summer season. Bessie, the senior cook, was asked to accompany other essential members of the household staff. Of course she was delighted to be in Ramsgate, she didn't like London at all in the heat of the summer. It was far too polluted and claustrophobic besides which her brother Jack had taken up a position as a guardsman several years ago when the new Ramsgate Sands Station had opened its doors back in 1863. Wealthy visitors to the town alighted at the new station which was situated conveniently just below the cliffs. Bessie looked forward to spending some of her precious time off with Jack and his large family.

The kitchen was down in the basement. Two young scullery maids assisted Bessie and they all shared tiny living quarters adjacent to the main kitchen area. It was cramped compared to the large house that Lord Frederick called home in The Royal Crescent near Holland Park, London. Bessie was in her early 40's, rotund and always waddling around because she carried far too much extra flesh. Spending most of her life in the kitchen, with easy access to food, was a problem. Her will was weak and she loved her homemade pies and fancy cakes. She was a kind, good woman by nature, but unfortunately easily taken advantage of by others. She could easily sense when people were suffering and she was always willing to help. She had been in service since the age of 14, never married but really loved and was utterly devoted to her long time employers, Lord Frederick and Lady Louise. She tried to help all the silly young servant girls if they got into trouble. When an old tramp came knocking at the servant's entrance, she would always see what she could rustle up from her kitchen's store cupboards and fill his billycan with hot soup.

Bessie was a woman of routine and order; she was particularly fastidious when it came to cleanliness. She insisted that her kitchen sparkled and that meant a lot of extra hard work scrubbing floors and work surfaces. Her greatest fear was food poisoning. Bessie would often say to the scullery maids, "If the household becomes sick I could lose my job and then where would I be?" She often dwelt upon such notions. She had no husband or wealthy family to fall back upon for support; her wellbeing and destiny was completely in her own hands. Over many years of working in domestic service she had come to her own conclusions. Food left lying around not only smelled bad but also it looked bad and when it was eaten sickness usually followed. Bessie had witnessed too many household staff complain of stomach pain followed quickly by nausea, sometimes vomiting and even diarrhoea. Often they would have to take to their bed for several days. She resolved that she would always maintain a clean kitchen. Her own careful observations had been confirmed in more recent years when George, the Butler, relayed what he had read in the London newspapers.

In 1847 there had been a Hungarian doctor called Ignaz Semmelweis who had advocated washing hands when delivering babies. He had noticed that the mother had a greater chance of avoiding childbed fever and often a premature death. Then in 1862 a chemist called Louis Pasteur had talked about *The Germ Theory of Disease* and

Bessie noted that it was only last year in 1867 that a man called Joseph Lister began to advocate that surgeons follow his lead and use antiseptics in surgery. This was all a bit above Bessie's head, her reading ability was limited and she didn't understand much of what George had shared at the staff dinner table but she did know, deep down in her own inner knowing, that her kitchen should be clean. She carefully selected only the freshest fish and meat when she shopped in the local market.

All this cleaning and cooking was a lot for Bessie to manage. She rose up early every morning and insisted upon visiting the markets herself to ensure the freshest foods. Ramsgate proved to be a whole new adventure, and there were new sights, sounds and smells. She waddled down Military Road to where the fishermen had their huts, and where the nets would be hanging out to dry. She always purchased the finest catch of the day that they could offer. Bessie was often tired, her work day was long and then there was all the extra pressure that she put upon herself to ensure that everything was perfect. She always worried about sickness and she particularly worried about Lady Louise. Her Ladyship was pale, frail and delicate. She reminded Bessie of a little bird that had fallen from the nest and was unable to fly. Lady Louise spent much of her time sleeping. When she was awake she was always in some kind of pain, perhaps her head, sometimes her joints and at other times her stomach. She didn't care much for food and seemed to be wasting away. Doctors had come and gone over the years and Bessie noticed that she always had a bottle of Laudanum on her nightstand.

Opium was widely available in 19th century Britain; it was even sold in barbers shops, ironmongers, confectioners, tobacconists and stationary establishments. It was easy to come by and prescribed for an alarming number of ailments for both children and adults. Laudanum, the most popular form, in which Opium was dissolved in alcohol was widely recommended in cases of fever, sleeplessness, tickly cough, biliousness, colic, cholera, diarrhoea and headaches. No one understood the concept of addiction but there was a growing awareness and concern amongst the medical community that something should be done to curb its availability. Medical Officers were becoming convinced that Opium was the major cause behind infantile death. Laudanum was marketed, as *Mother's Little Helper* and mothers would use it to quiet a cough, colic or a screaming baby. The baby was kept in a state of continued narcosis and as a consequence refused food or proper nourishment. Laudanum caused many children under the age of five to starve to death.

Over the years that she had been in service Bessie had witnessed Lady Louise's painful demise and she knew that Opium was the problem. She also witnessed many friends and colleagues of Lord Frederick fall into a similar habit. There were notorious Opium dens in the east end of London where men would gather to smoke. George and the other household lads had told her all about them. Bessie saw people struggling in poverty, often she would have to step over men lying in the streets in an Opium induced coma. A bottle of Laudanum was often by their side. There was nothing good about the substance; it was associated with a fall from grace, criminal activity and ultimately an untimely death. She experienced a lot of pain herself. Her knees weren't in the best of health and neither was her back. She had a lot of general aches and pains, and being so rotund did not help. She was out of breath much of the time as she waddled along. Of course there had always been the temptation to buy some Laudanum when her pain was particularly bad but a deep inner knowing always stayed Bessie's hand from venturing down a path best not traveled.

Bessie was particularly proud of Lord Frederick. She loved to see him in his deep red silk smoking jacket embellished with two dragons facing each other. She knew that he enjoyed Turkish tobacco. Thanks to the Crimean War back in the 1850's Turkish tobacco had become hugely popular in Britain. After dinner he would don his jacket and retreat into the billiards room with the other male dinner guests. The jacket absorbed most of the smell of the smoke and protected his clothes from falling ash. Bessie also knew that he favoured the Turkish tobacco and declined the Opium, which was a Godsend. Sometimes she noticed Lord Frederick weeping quietly when he thought no one was observing. He was so saddened and perplexed by his wife's demise; she had fallen into a world of sleep and shadows and he lamented that he had lost his sweetheart and friend.

1868 was an important year because Bessie knew that her employer was very busy and engaged in some special work at The House of Lords in London. There had been much debate in government circles that something must be done about the easy availability of poisonous substances. Currently the only controlled substance was arsenic. There had been much talk that the British Government was preparing to pass a Pharmacy Act sometime over the summer. 15 dangerous substances had been named and would be classified as poisonous. Opium was included late in the day because many chemists and druggists depended upon the sale of Laudanum to sustain their business. When George had conveyed to her what he had recently read in the newspapers she was extremely relieved. Bessie knew in her heart that controlling these substances might curb other innocent adults and children falling by the wayside. As for Lady Louise, Bessie wondered if it was all too late. Time was running out for her Ladyship but Bessie resolved to help her in any way that she could. Perseverance was one of her finest characteristics and while there was still hope Bessie would not give up.

She decided that she needed to ask for help. Bessie had never been a regular church attendee. Christmas and Eastertide were the only two occasions when she felt compelled to attend a service; she preferred to spend Sundays out in the open air if she had the choice. In any case she wasn't exactly sure how one prayed or if she was doing it correctly, but deep in her inner knowing she knew it was the right thing to do. On the first Sunday in July Bessie donned her Sunday best jacket, her straw hat with long flowing silk ribbons and gloves and ventured into the town to attend the morning service at St Georges. The church had been built in 1824 and its enormous west tower with its lantern turret was an imposing landmark, the ships used it for navigational purposes. She liked the idea of asking for help here after all St George had slain the dragon and as far as Bessie was concerned dragons symbolized the dark, shadowy world of Opium. George had told her all about the Opium wars and how the Chinese were so addicted to the drug. She didn't remember much of the service, and the church was crowded. Bessie simply looked up to the heavens above and asked with all of her heart and soul for some guidance.

Surprisingly it came in the form of chocolate cake! Bessie had a strange dream that night and it was the chocolate cake that jolted her memory the next morning when she woke up. She was restless in bed, it was hot and stuffy and particularly oppressive in her tiny bedroom. In her dream she was in her Ramsgate kitchen making a chocolate cake, one of her favourite recipes. She had just taken a teaspoon of the cake mix to sample when the scullery maid's attention was directed elsewhere and was in the process of savoring every moment. Suddenly she became aware that a stranger had joined her. She was a roly-poly old lady with a wizened face. The woman had the audacity to dip her own spoon into the cake mix! Before Bessie could object the old woman began to talk in urgent tones, "I know that you want to help Lady Louise, you have a good heart, and I can help you. Listen carefully, take George with you and venture into the town. There is a homoeopathic chemist shop on the High Street, please be sure to ask for the chemist's help to break her Opium habit. There are remedies that can assist. Take the bottle of Laudanum away; she will be very difficult for a long time but you must persevere. Give her some strong black coffee, as this will wake her up. She is between the worlds, you must bring her back, it's not her time yet, and she still has good work to do. She will be very sick, probably lots of nausea, vomiting, maybe diarrhoea, headaches, muscle ache and pains. Bessie, you should sit with her, hold her hand through the darkness, she may be very frightened and she may see awful things. You must do this, have faith and patience and in the end all will be well."

Bessie was about to open her mouth, but in a flash the old woman had disappeared. She recalled the vivid dream because she always remembered dreams about food, especially when cake was involved. She reflected for a long time upon the old woman's message. It compelled her to take George aside the next day and share all that happened and about her concern for Lady Louise. Together they decided to pay the homoeopathic chemist a visit when they had a chance.

The following day offered the ideal opportunity as Lord Frederick was up in London attending to government business and Lady Louise lay in a narcotic induced comatose state. Bessie and George ventured into Ramsgate High Street and easily found the homoeopathic chemist and druggist. An ancient but kind, trust worthy sort of gentleman greeted them and spent considerable time listening to their story and plea for help. He knew all too well the horrors of Laudanum dependency and eventually he offered them several small vials of remedies, they were tiny white pills in small glass bottles with a cork stopper. He told them that they might assist with Lady Louise's recovery. He confirmed exactly what the old lady in Bessie's chocolate cake dream had told her, "It's likely that she will not be well for some time. She will probably experience nausea, vomiting, diarrhoea, muscle ache and pains and terrible night terrors. It will be a dark time for you all, but take courage; these little vials will help you to navigate through to the other side. Please don't give up. I have witnessed these remedies work miracles; they are God's gift to us in our time of greatest need." The old gentleman also offered George the leather bound book, *Homoeopathic Domestic Medicine* written by Joseph Laurie MD and published by James Leath in 1854. "This book will guide you." George studied the labels on the four small vials resting in the palm of his hand: *Ipec, Belladonna, Nux Vomica and Mercurius.* The old gentleman found the appropriate page in the leather bound book relating to poisons and the vices of Laudanum and explained how the remedies might assist.

The two friends returned to the Ramsgate villa with a spring in their step and with greater conviction and more confidence that they would succeed in bringing Lady Louise back to life. They shared their knowledge and plan with the rest of the household staff and it was decided that they would all take action the next day. Elsie, Lady Louise's lady's maid, removed the bottle of Laudanum from her nightstand and all the other bottles that she found hidden in the bedroom cupboards, drawers and in the bathroom. A large bowl was placed beside her bed and Bessie brewed some strong coffee in the kitchen to wake her up. George carefully studied the homoeopathic book. It was not going to be a pretty picture. The strong coffee woke her up and her Ladyship was fine for a few hours but then she didn't feel well and begun to search earnestly for her Laudanum. When she couldn't find her comfort medicine the living hell begun. With Lord Frederick busy in London the household took control. Initially the small vial of *Ipec* helped with her nausea, vomiting and angry outbursts. When she developed a high fever and experienced terrible hallucinations and night terrors the little vial called *Belladonna* seemed to work wonders. When her mouth was covered in ulcers and she began to drool excessively all over the bedclothes George said to use the *Mercurius.* When she ranted and raved and had severe constipation sometimes alternating with diarrhoea they used *Nux Vomica.* The leather bound book became their Bible. Bessie and Elsie took turns to sit with Lady Louise to ensure that she was never left alone. In the end it was the love and dedication of the whole household that brought her through all the turmoil, pain and terror.

After three weeks they were done, the storm was finally over. Lady Louise woke up one morning and asked Elsie to dress her and then she requested to take her breakfast in the dining room. Breakfast was followed by a stroll along the east cliff promenade in Ramsgate with Elsie by her side. The sky was the most beautiful blue, the sun shimmered on the sea, gulls reeled overhead and for the first time in many years Lady Louise felt that she had recovered her soul. All of her broken pieces were mended. Bessie smiled and muttered to herself, "Today I will make a chocolate cake to celebrate." They were all weary but every member of the household knew that they had made a difference. With the help of some strange white pills her Ladyship had finally found safe harbour in Ramsgate.

Lord Frederick was absolutely thrilled to see that his sweetheart had returned to a healthier state. His 1868 Pharmacy Bill was passed into law and he always remembered his Ramsgate household with great affection and notable generosity. Five years later he was offered a position as British Ambassador in The Americas. It was finally time for Bessie and George to move on. Since that summer in 1868 they had become close friends and now George asked for her hand in marriage. They had both fallen in love with Ramsgate and planned to purchase a small business, a teashop, with living accommodation above. To their astonishment and delight Lord Frederick and Lady Louise bought the premises for them as a wedding gift. Lord Frederick couldn't forget how much they had both helped in his wife's recovery and road to better health and for that he was eternally grateful.

As they were all helping to pack up the London household Bessie came across Lord Frederick's red smoking jacket with the gold and black dragons facing each other. She asked if she could keep it as a timely reminder of the family and that auspicious summer spent in Ramsgate back in 1868. The teashop was a great success; everyone loved Bessie's homemade cakes especially the chocolate ones. However, under George's eagle eye and her newfound love she mustered up the will power to finally resist over indulgence and eventually lost her excess weight. Bessie's shapelier figure brought with it better health, increased energy and a newfound joy. The villa where they had all spent the summer of 1868 was now part of the exclusive Granville Hotel. All eight villas were converted in 1869 into a hotel and it attracted a wealth of visitors during the season. Many guests ventured into the High Street and enjoyed afternoon tea at Bessie and George's establishment. Tea and cake were served with love and gratitude for many of life's blessings.

Poppy opened her eyes. She fingered the red silk smoking jacket smiled and whispered to Jack the Lad, "What a wonderful story, Bessie and George's kindness and perseverance helped a very sick lady overcome adversity and the almost impossible task of kicking a drug habit." Poppy was all too familiar with the evil hold that Opiates have in present times. She had recently read a newspaper report announcing alarming figures. She knew that the USA has been in the grip of an Opioid epidemic since the 1990's but more and more deaths were now happening in England. Poppy had observed this first hand when she had lived up in London. Newspapers continued to report that the prescription of Opioids by GP's in England has steadily risen, especially in more deprived communities. *The Telegraph* had reported back in March 2018 that the number of prescriptions for powerful painkillers in England had nearly doubled over the past 10 years. According to the BBC some 28.3 million Opioids were prescribed by GP's in 2017 to treat severe pain. Poppy sighed and once again began to reflect upon her own name, she glanced across at the lovely wall painting that Cedric's artist friend had painted for her, beautiful red poppies blowing in the wind.

Poppy was all too familiar with pain. She had felt a lot of physical pain over her 51 years, especially her knees and her back but it was the emotional pain that had really cut her down. She had experienced periods of sorrow and deep despair, anger and frustration, feelings of isolation, sensations of not belonging and being excluded. Yes, they were all familiar bedfellows and they all brought pain in one-way or another. Poppy could identify with Lady Louise and wondered what mental and emotional problems may have led to her own cycle of physical pain. Many headaches, backache and stomach problems had obviously led to Lady Louise's dependency upon a little bottle of Laudanum waiting patiently upon her bed stand for her next fix. "But what was behind it all?" Poppy asked Jack the Lad. She reflected that the problems of yesterday seemed just as important and pervasive as those of today and in fact the passage time had changed nothing at all. In reality Opium addiction was and still is a huge problem. Poppy gently fingered the two embroidered dragons and her mind turned to Dr. Edward Bach and his little book, *The Twelve Healers.* The little tattered booklet had appeared in a pile of old dressmaking patterns and fashion magazines that had been left on the doorstep of the Margate shop. Poppy opened the book up and reminded herself of the things that she had read in the spring. The opening lines were so intriguing:

This system of treatment is the most perfect, which has been given to mankind within living memory. It has the power to cure disease, and, in its simplicity, it may be used in the household.

As Poppy continued to read she learnt that the system of healing set out in the little booklet had been Divinely revealed, a Gift from God, showing that our fears, our cares, our anxieties, likes and dislikes, greed, indecision and such like are the things that open the path to the invasion of illness. Poppy learnt that the Herbs given to us by the Grace of the Creator could take away the fears and worries and would leave us happier and better in ourselves and in doing so the disease, no matter what it is, would leave.

The remedies of Nature given in this book have proved that that they are blest above others in their work of mercy; and that they have been given the power to heal all types of illness and suffering.

As Poppy continued to read she was reminded of all that had happened in her first year working for Madam Popoff. Many customers who crossed the threshold of the Madam Popoff Vintage Emporium had some sort of ailment and she recalled how over the past year she had noticed that those who spent time in the back room with Madam seemed to do a lot better. In fact so many returned just to thank Madam that Poppy had often wondered if Madam knew all about this system of healing introduced by Dr. Edward Bach.

Take no notice of the disease, think only of the outlook on life of the one in distress.

Poppy had begun to understand that it was important to treat the personality and not the disease. Treat the state of mind or the moods and with the return to normal, the disease, whatever it might be, would go away too. Poppy found this all to be extremely fascinating. She had become privy to so many life stories during her sojourn at the Madam Popoff

Vintage Emporium and now she was learning how people could be helped in their sufferings. She knew so many people who had undergone counselling over the years, including herself, but still remained stuck in their own traumas, dramas and sickness. Poppy smiled to herself. Edward Bach had arrived to open a new door in her life and Poppy had embarked upon a whole new adventure!

The little booklet continued to describe *The Twelve Healers* and recommended the following herbs:

* ***Agrimony*** for cheerful people who like to joke and laugh and cannot cope with arguments or quarrels, these are carefully avoided, they worry and can feel restless and tormented by their troubles but these are always carefully hidden behind good humour. They tend to use alcohol and drugs to help them keep up the façade of cheerfulness.

* ***Centaury*** would apparently be beneficial for quiet, gentle people who are over anxious to help and serve other people and whose good nature often results in them doing much more than their fair share of the work, so much so that they may neglect their own mission in life.

Poppy had seen many aspects of this remedy in her own life story. She had always wanted to help others. She knew it was important to be kind and helpful; after all they were such noble traits. She had always been taught this growing up, but she did realize that other people had perceived her weakness and her inability to set healthy boundaries. Consequently many had taken advantage. Poppy knew that she found it very difficult to say, "NO" and realized that her own weakness had set herself up for situations that caused her grief, anger and festering resentment.

Poppy could also see many aspects of *Centaury* in Bessie's personality. She was a kind, helpful, compassionate lady but she had a very weak will especially when it came to food, particularly cakes and sweets! Poppy was glad that George had taken her in hand and their blossoming love affair had finally helped Bessie to become stronger and able to resist temptation. As a bonus her weight and overall health had improved.

* ***Cerato*** for those who don't have sufficient confidence in themselves to make their own decisions, constantly ask advice from others and are often misguided.

Poppy had also seen that aspects of this remedy matched her own personality but since she had been gainfully employed at the Madam Popoff Vintage Emporium and more recently in her own Ramsgate shop she felt that she was becoming stronger in her own mind. She was definitely more decisive and had begun to call upon her own inner wisdom.

* ***Chicory*** for those who are over mindful of the needs of others and tend to be over full of care for children, relatives and friends. They are always trying to find something to put right. They are possessive people, they want their loved ones near and enjoy correcting things they consider wrong. They are apt to become fussy and agitated in their care for others.

* ***Clematis*** could be recommended for those who are dreamy, drowsy, and not fully awake and who have no great interest in life. Quiet people, who are not really happy in their present circumstances, live more in the future than in the present. In illness some make little effort to get well, and in certain cases may even look forward to death because they might meet again some loved one whom they have lost.

Poppy smiled and immediately thought about Lady Louise. She had spent so much of her time under the influence of Laudanum. She had been asleep or semi-conscious and wandered around lost in a shadowy grey world. Poppy was so very pleased to know that Madam Popoff had stepped in to help; she knew in her heart that it was she who had appeared in the chocolate cake dream to Bessie and offered the gift of homoeopathic remedies. "*Clematis* would have helped too," Poppy muttered to herself.

* ***Gentian*** for those who are easily discouraged. They may be progressing well in illness or in the affairs of their daily life but don't do well if there is a small delay or hindrance to progress, as they soon become doubtful and disheartened.

* ***Impatiens*** for those who are quick in thought and action and who wish all things to be done without hesitation or delay. When they are ill they are anxious for a hasty recovery. They don't like slow people and they often prefer to work alone so that they can get everything done at their own speed.

Poppy knew a lot of people who probably needed this particular remedy! It would have definitely helped her many colleagues from the past when she had worked in a busy London office. Some of the customers who had crossed the threshold of the Madam Popoff Vintage Emporium needed this remedy and then there were the dogs. Jack the Lad was always so impatient, always urging her onto Ramsgate, Ship Shape Café, Winston and the sausages. Poppy decided that she would purchase a bottle and try it out on her devoted little companion.

* ***Mimulus*** for those who are fearful. It is for the fear of everyday life, of worldly things such as illness, pain, accidents, poverty, of the dark, of being alone, and of misfortune. These people quietly keep these things to themselves and don't speak about their fears to others.

Poppy knew this would also be a good remedy for herself, so many of her friends told her that she needed more courage especially in the love department! She decided that if she was going to try things out on Jack the Lad that she would purchase some ***Mimulus*** for herself. She reflected upon the story of the smoking jacket and thought that Bessie would have benefited from this remedy too; she had always been worried about things, particularly cleanliness and concern about illness.

* ***Rock Rose*** the remedy for emergency, where there appears to be no hope. In accident or sudden illness, or when the patient is very frightened or terrified.

Poppy reflected upon Lady Louise, in her darkest moments, when the household was helping her to detoxify from her Laudanum dependency, and said to herself, "Surely she would have benefited from this remedy. She experienced such terrifying hallucinations."

* ***Scleranthus*** for those who suffer much from being unable to decide between two things, first one seeming right then the other. They are usually quiet people, and bear their difficulty alone, as they are not inclined to discuss it with others.

* ***Vervain*** for those with fixed principles and ideas, which they are confident are right, and which they rarely change. They have a great wish to convert all those around to their own views of life. They have a strong will and like to teach. This is a remedy for over enthusiasm and a strained state of mind.

* ***Water Violet*** for those who in health and illness like to be alone. Very quiet people who move about without noise, speak little and then gently. They are very independent, capable and self-reliant and almost free of the opinions of others. They are aloof, leave people alone and go their own way. Water Violet types are often clever and talented. Their peace and calmness is a blessing to those around them.

Poppy sighed; she could see so many of her own friends, the customers at the Madam Popoff Vintage Emporium, people from her past, herself included in these remedy pictures. Then there were so many of the people whose lives had come to her through the things that she had handled in the shop, at one time or another they too may have benefited from one or more of these *Twelve Healers.*

She put the little tattered book carefully back in her bag knowing that this was her most important treasure. That evening back in the warm confines of Lookout Retreat Poppy shared the story of the red smoking jacket with Aunt Flora. They also discussed at great length the current drug problem, which sadly was always in the local news. Aunt Flora had plenty to say on the subject, "The Isle of Thanet area, which covers the towns of Margate, Ramsgate and Broadstairs, has a big drug problem Poppy. One sees people openly dealing in the town centres and bars and what's even more distressing is the use of young children to do the dirty work of those further up the food chain. I'm not sure what the answer is; I know the situation has fuelled much local debate. So many young lives are wasted when addiction takes hold."

Poppy decided that she really must give the Bach flower remedies a try and debated whether she should purchase a complete set; she had recently discovered that there were 38 in total. Continuing to extend her knowledge and to read more about the life and work of Dr. Bach felt so right. "Aunt Flora I really do think that these flower remedies can help people with their mental and emotional states, perhaps help to get them to a better place. I believe that if I continue to study this system I can help those people who come into the shop looking for much more than simply an item of vintage clothing."

Chapter 4

Poppy and Aunt Flora had recently watched the new Mary Poppins film over at the Palace Cinema in Harbour Street, Broadstairs. The Palace is a tiny family run business with only 111 seats, quaint and reminiscence of bygone days when cinemas were small and there was only one screen.

According to Mary Poppins there's only one way to go and that's up. Poppy had this on her mind when she opened up the Ramsgate shop early one windy and wet day in early November. Jack the Lad was glad to be out of the cold wind; Poppy fetched an old towel from the tiny back room and rubbed his sodden coat dry. As he made himself comfortable on his velvet cushion she brought in a large oblong cardboard box wrapped in a black dustbin liner that had been left on the doorstep.

Poppy never knew what to expect when people had been clearing out their attics and basements. She had become privy to so many stories over the past year working in Madam Popoff's employment; these unwanted treasures carried memories, often good ones but some memories were best left undisturbed. There really wasn't much inside the long cardboard box. Poppy pulled out a decorative string of bunting fashioned from small faded cotton union flags. However, underneath the bunting was a rather large and distinguished looking black umbrella with a beautiful elegant ivory handle carved in the shape of a swan's head. As Poppy continued to examine her newly discovered treasure she noticed a little gold plate attached to the base of the ivory handle. It was beautifully engraved in italics. She read the name, *Henry* and the date *1890.* The umbrella was in particularly good condition; obviously it had been well loved and cared for.

The shop was quiet, it was gloomy and wet outside and there were few visitors in the town. Poppy settled down with a cup of tea and laid the umbrella on her lap, she began to finger the elegant ivory handle and as she shut her eyes she was quickly transported back to another time.

Henry was smart and wealthy; he came from a well to do Ramsgate family of merchants. His successful father had funded both Henry's private school and university education and helped him launch his career as a Ramsgate solicitor. Henry always remembered the day that his mother had presented him with the elegant umbrella. He had recently passed his solicitors examinations, his future looked bright and rosy and he was about to marry an eligible Ramsgate beauty. His marriage was more a matter of pleasing his parents than of his own choosing. Maud came from a good family, she was pretty and on the surface she seemed to be a very suitable choice but it really wasn't a marriage made in heaven. Most of the time they just weren't on the same page. Maud was vivacious and fun, an extrovert and loved to socialize. Henry, on the other hand, was quiet, hardworking, studious and distinguished. He preferred the companionship of his oak clad study and the comfort of his large collection of books when he returned home from a busy day at his law office.

Much to his wife's relief everything changed when their first and only child was born in 1894. They named him Hugh. Henry's baby son lit up his life and he began to spend more time with his son and wife. Father and son became inseparable, Henry doted on him and as Hugh grew older they would spend hours reading and playing together with Hugh's large basket of wooden toys. The boy was clever, quick to learn and privileged just like his father. The family lived in a respectable Regency period home in Wellington Crescent. Their home was situated high up on the east cliff of Ramsgate overlooking the sea and the busy harbour.

Eventually Hugh was sent to St Lawrence College, a private Ramsgate school with an excellent academic record. He excelled both in his studies and on the rugby field. Father and son were inquisitive and both shared an interest in science. They loved to read and discuss the latest scientific research or wonder together at the many inventions of the day. They read all about the exploits of the Wright brothers in Kitty Hawk, North Carolina on December 17th 1903. Kitty Hawk had been chosen because of its high winds. Hugh was only nine years old at the time but to a young boy this was absolutely magical. Man could actually fly like a bird. Hugh looked up towards the sky in wonder. Of course Henry didn't know it at the time and neither did Hugh; but sadly this was to mark the beginning of the end. Six years later, when he was fifteen, the Wright brothers had become quite famous. The brothers travelled to France in 1909 with their ideas and inventions. They were entertained and sought after by nobility and heads of state and were actively selling their airplanes.

Hugh became obsessed with flight; it was the talk of the century, cutting edge technology, adventurous and the stuff of dreams. He was determined to become an aviator. Each time his father opened up his umbrella Hugh would squeeze Henry's arm tightly and look deep into his eyes. With great conviction he would announce that there was only one way to go and that was upwards. These words haunted Henry; he heard them replay on the rainy days when he opened up his elegant black umbrella.

In the early spring of 1912 Hugh turned 18. As a special birthday surprise Henry and Maud presented him with a large box. Much to Hugh's delight he found a model aircraft carefully wrapped in tissue paper alongside a receipt for 12 flying lessons at the Aero Club in Eastchurch on the Isle of Sheppey in Kent. Hugh was excited and extremely grateful because his wildest dreams were about to become a reality.

Flying from Eastchurch first began in 1909 when the Short Brothers, well known for their interest in aircraft, built a glider that took off from Stamford Hill. Frank McClean had acquired Stonepits Farm on the marshes and subsequently he converted 400 acres of land into an airfield. The airfield eventually developed into a home to the wealthy flying fraternity. Later Mr. McClean loaned the airplanes based at Eastchurch to the Royal Navy to train officers in the skill of flying. Royal Naval Air Service Eastchurch existed from June 1913 until 1st April 1918 when the Royal Naval Air Service and the Royal Flying Corps combined to form the Royal Air Force.

Hugh took to the skies like a duck to water. He was enthusiastic, quick to learn, confident and popular with his instructors and the members of the Aero Club. Within six months he had become an accomplished pilot. He had honed all of his flying skills and was well respected amongst his peer group and the senior members of the Aero Club.

Completing his pilot training coincided with his graduation from school. There was much debate within the family circle as to where Hugh should direct his future. Henry wanted him to go up to Oxford. He was a bright, popular young man with a glowing future ahead of him. Maud could see that her son would not be happy cooped up in academia. She rather wanted him to be a free spirit. Hugh himself felt that the sky was calling him, he felt complete when he was up in the air. He loved to be high up in the clouds with a bird's eye view. At the controls of his little plane he was able to survey the patchwork of green fields, forests and toy town settlements.

A Naval Air Training School had already become established at Eastchurch in 1912 however; Hugh was interested in joining the Royal Flying Corps. It became active on April 13th, 1912. His maternal grandfather had been an army man and Hugh was eager to continue in the family tradition. Henry wasn't happy about the situation; an army career and one that was based in the air really didn't fulfil the vision he had for his only child. Every time that Henry opened up his elegant black umbrella he was reminded of his son's urgent plea, "Father the only way to go is up."

In the end he threw in the towel and gave into his son's dream. Henry didn't have the heart to encourage Hugh to follow a different path. He knew that his son had his life all mapped out, yearning for the sky and Henry knew deep in his heart that it was fruitless to keep his only son tethered. He just had to let him go. Hugh was fit, healthy, well educated, and clever. As a trained pilot he would make a perfect officer in the Royal Flying Corps.

When the war broke out on the 4th August 1914 Henry naturally feared for his son's safety. Local boys were signing up and everyone thought that it would all be over by Christmas. No one predicted how long it would last and the utter devastation that would follow in its wake. A seaplane base had been established at St. Mildred's Bay Westgate - on - Sea during the summer of 1914. Over time, as the base developed, Henry would regularly take the train from Ramsgate to Margate; he walked past The Royal Sea Bathing Hospital and along the cliffs towards the base. In his spare time he would spend hours watching the seaplane activity. He watched the men wade out and help the planes out to sea and observed the experienced pilots manoeuvre in inclement weather. This was his special place where he felt closest to Hugh. He never knew where his son was but Henry speculated that on most days he was probably on a mission with the Royal Flying Corps protecting the Kent coast. In April 1915 an airfield on the adjacent chalk cliff top was created. Henry watched the Sopwith Babies and the Short 184's and saw in his mind's eye his son up above defending his country. Every time that he opened his black umbrella he heard his son's voice, "Father the only way to go is up!" Henry smiled and always prayed to God for his son's safe passage.

Zeppelin raids were bringing war directly to English civilians. Daylight bombing raids by German Gotha Bombers caused havoc. Ramsgate was the most bombed town in the United Kingdom during the Great War. The Royal Flying Corps were now very well established and took an active part in defence. The Handley Page Bomber was often seen in the skies over Margate, Ramsgate and Broadstairs because a bomber training school had opened at the newly established Manston Aerodrome.

Henry and Maud never knew what really happened. The news came with the telegraph boy around Christmas 1917. The sight of a young boy approaching the home was every parent's nightmare. A telegram always heralded bad news: unbearable news. Hugh was missing in action, he was presumed dead. His aircraft was nowhere to be found. For months Henry scanned the skies in his daytime waking and in his restless dreams. He looked to the heavens above for answers, he ranted and raved when no one was at home and he often slipped quietly into the ancient St. Laurence - In - Thanet Church where he and Maud worshipped. Inside the sanctity of the church he asked God many questions, "Why? When? Where?" No answers were ever forthcoming, only the still black night of despair prevailed. In the end Henry had to accept that his beloved son was gone.

Maud didn't want to get out of bed she had lost her compass. No matter what anyone said or did she just couldn't pull herself together and move on. Henry's elegant black umbrella was wrapped in tissue and banished to the attic. Sadly, the angel of death knocked yet again on Wellington Crescent in the autumn of 1918. An H1 influenza virus had been circulating amongst humans since 1900 and it had picked up genetic material from a bird flu virus just before 1918. As a consequence a deadly pandemic strain was about to wreak havoc on a world ripe with trauma and grief. When the damage was over 50 million people worldwide would be dead, globally three times the number that fell upon The Great War battlefields. In Britain alone 228,000, a quarter of the population, died from what became known as *The Spanish Influenza.*

Maud was severely depressed so it was easy for the killer virus to take hold and attack her already compromised immune system. It all began quickly with a fever, aching muscles, chills, sweats and a headache. Soon a debilitating cough took over together with fatigue and weakness. Finally opportunistic bacteria attacked her lungs and caused the dreaded pneumonia. When Henry observed his wife coughing up blood he knew that she was done for. Her grip on life had been tenuous since Hugh's disappearance, now she was ready to let go and join him in the stars.

Losing Maud ate away at Henry's mind and body. Grief was like an acid gnawing at the very fabric of his being. He had lost the two most important people in his life. Only a great void remained. When the Armistice Day bells tolled at the eleventh hour on the eleventh day of the eleventh month Henry had nothing to celebrate. He tasted only the bitter pill of resentment, grief and loss. He knew that he was not alone. Many families had lost their loved ones. Grief had torn them apart and Ramsgate would never be the same, as a whole generation of young men had been lost. Henry looked to the stars and knew that his own life on earth would never be the same.

Help eventually came in the form of Constance his older sister. She appeared on his doorstep without invitation just before Christmas 1918. She had an enormous suitcase, three hatboxes and a little fluffy dog. Constance was a force to be reckoned with, a fiery lady, full of confidence and wit. From her large home in central London she had held court over a number of years. All the fashionable and passionate ladies of Kensington knew Constance. She was a leading light in the women's suffrage movement. Like Henry, she was well educated and clever. A successful marriage to a wealthy banker who had been happy to give his wife a free rein meant that Constance had both the time and the money to devote her life to women's issues. In 1918, when young men were dying on the battlefields, Constance and her friends celebrated a monumental act of parliament. Women over the age of thirty were granted the vote. They had to be either householders, wives of householders, or women who occupied a property with an annual rent of five pounds or more. The vote was also granted to women who were graduates of a British university.

At the conclusion of her successful work in London's politics Henry's sister now had time to help him. Underneath it all she had a very big and sensitive heart. She could feel her brother's pain and anguish and knew that she would lose him if she sat by and did nothing. That Christmas she devoted her every waking moment to his care. She ensured that he ate, exercised and didn't hide away in his oak clad study. She talked to him, shared fond memories of Hugh and Maud and helped him to realize that the clocks on earth were still ticking. He was still here and had a higher purpose, important work to do. Henry began to sense the cold winds and waves that swept in from the sea whispering his name and calling him. One night, in that new spirit of openness, Henry's higher purpose eventually revealed itself in a dream.

He was flying high up in the clouds, not in an aircraft, but with his own golden wings. He found himself in Belgium flying over the wasted land. He saw the broken bodies, the vast holes left by shellfire and he smelled the stench if it all. He could see that so many young men had no final resting place in this barren desert. Their own loved ones, just like himself, had no idea where they lay. There was no place for them to go to reflect and mourn. There was no closure. As he headed back home and flew over Beachy Head Lighthouse, the cliff tops and the Sussex down lands the bright yellow *gorse* bushes soothed his troubled spirit and gave him a sense of hope.

The next day at breakfast, reading his daily newspaper, Henry digested an article that changed the course of his life. The article described the work of Mr. Fabian Ware and the War Graves Commission. As Henry continued to read he was reminded of his dream and immediately knew deep in his heart that with his own skills and connections he would make a perfect volunteer. At long last he could be of some use; an opportunity had presented itself to channel his grief into something positive and uplifting.

At the age of forty-five Fabian Ware was too old to fight in the Great War but he became commander of a Red Cross Mobile Unit. The human slaughter that he had observed first hand drove him into action. He wanted to ensure that the final resting places of the dead would not be lost forever so his unit began to document and care for the graves that they could find. By 1915 this work was officially recognized and later encouraged and expanded by the patronage of the Prince of Wales. By 1918 587,000 graves had been identified and a further 559,000 casualties were registered as having no known graves. Prominent architects of the day were chosen to design and construct cemeteries and memorials. The famous author, Rudyard Kipling, whose son John remained missing presumed dead, was given the job of literary advisor and asked to recommend suitable inscriptions.

Henry directed his grief into purposeful activity and in doing so he found the energy to get up and out of bed every day. He carried on and in the process he made new friends and acquaintances. Of course nothing could ever replace his much-loved son and the emptiness of a large home without his wife. Knowing that so many families were suffering a similar fate, but with the knowledge that his new work was offering solace, it was enough for Henry to continue and to complete his own life's journey. In his quiet moments he acknowledged that one had to look upon the bright side. As the years marched on he learnt to celebrate small blessings. He acknowledged his comfortable home, his friends, his sister and her family and the important work that he had accomplished with the War Graves Commission.

It was a life well lived. Henry never discovered what had happened to Hugh. Often when he gazed out across the Ramsgate cliffs he sensed that he could hear Hugh's whisper upon the wind, "Father the only way to go is up." Henry would smile and shout out towards the horizon, “Yes son, so it is!”

Poppy opened her eyes, she had been crying. Her hands gently patted the elegant black umbrella with its striking ivory handle carved into the head and neck of a swan. She knew that it had been hidden away, wrapped in the fading tissue paper, in some attic for over a hundred years. It had its own special but very sad story. She examined the ivory handle and the little gold plate that read, Henry *1890*. Poppy sighed to herself, “This umbrella certainly has a chequered history, and it oozes sadness.” She turned to Jack the Lad and announced, “We can’t sell this in the shop; it comes with far too much baggage.

Poppy began to reflect upon the forthcoming Armistice Day celebrations. This year, 2018, was particularly poignant as it marked the one-hundredth year anniversary of the ending of The Great War. Royal British Legion members and volunteers had been out in the town with their collecting tins and trays of poppies. She reflected once again upon her own name and thought about Henry, Maud and Hugh. Suddenly Poppy had an idea that felt the right thing to do. “I’ll donate this piece of history to one of the local museums. There’s always a need for displays, an elegant umbrella reminiscent of another time will complete a nice display somewhere.”

In the end it was just another day at the shop for Poppy and Jack the Lad but she also knew deep down in her heart that she was beginning to fully comprehend life and to understand what it means to be human. There are joys and celebrations but sometimes there's awful pain and suffering. Her mind turned to Dr. Edward Bach and his little tattered booklet, *The Twelve Healers.* A friend had recently shared with her the additional remedies that had followed the initial twelve. *The Seven Helpers* were new remedies to learn about and study.

Apparently *The Seven Helpers* are chronic conditions, emotional states which have developed over time; they may have become habitual and might make it more difficult to perceive which one of *The Twelve Healers* is really needed. Poppy had read with interest these new remedy states.

Olive - is for those people who are pale, worn out and exhausted. Their skin may be dry and wrinkled.

Vine - the vine flowers have no petals and this shows a lack of emotional sensitivity. For those who lack empathy towards others and how they feel may need *vine.* These people may have a high colour.

Rock Water - is for those people who take life too seriously.

Heather - is for people who talk too much about themselves. The buttonholers!

Wild Oat - is for those who are undecided as to the direction that they should take in life.

Gorse - is for people who may have a sallow complexion and dark rings around the eyes. *Gorse* is for those who have given up hope.

Oak - is for those people who struggle on regardless of the warning signs that they are damaging their health.

Gorse for a sense of hopelessness, a feeling that nothing else can be done to make things better particularly caught her attention. Poppy recalled Henry's dream where he was flying over the battlefields of France and Belgium and how he had turned for home and flew over the thickets of gorse bushes on the South Downs. She wondered if the bright yellow gorse bushes had been a catalyst for his healing. Perhaps they had influenced him to eventually move on from a place of inertia to a place of possibilities, a place to look up to and to spread his wings. "The only way to go is up," Poppy murmured to Jack the Lad and in her heart she sensed that Mary Poppins and Hugh were right. "Yes, upwards and onwards really is the only way to go!"

Chapter 5

Christmas was approaching. Poppy really enjoyed decorating the two large picture windows of her Ramsgate shop. She had purchased a small fir tree from the Ramsgate market and also picked up a few boxes of old sparkly baubles from a charity shop up in the High Street. Poppy loved sparkly things, they were so uplifting and made her feel very happy; Henry's story had left her with such a heavy heart. It was

December 6th, St Nicholas Day and Poppy recalled how in Holland shoes are left on the doorstep for St Nicholas to fill with treats and small toys for the children. She arrived with Jack the Lad in tow; it was an early frosty morning and she was most surprised to find a package discreetly tucked to one side on the doorstep underneath a copy of the local paper. Poppy opened up the shop, turned on the storage heaters and made herself a cup of coffee, she was eager to settle down in her armchair and see what St Nick had left her. The package was small and wrapped in sturdy brown paper. There was a very old tattered booklet of piano music and a small ring box. Poppy gasped as she opened the box. Inside, glowing on a velvety cushion was the most beautiful gold ring. It was fashioned into the shape of a turtle. His shell was made from a lovely green opal surrounded by seed pearls and his head was made from a large diamond. “Oh my!” exclaimed Poppy. She gently lifted it from the velvet cushion, examined it carefully with her long slender fingers, clutched it close to her heart and drifted back to another time.

As Florence alighted from the Ramsgate train she knew that she was late, she glanced down at her pretty wristwatch. It was seven o’clock. She had approximately fifteen minutes to rush along the Margate seafront and settle herself in front of the piano at Margate’s Hippodrome Theatre. She was a single mother, playing the piano for the silent movies brought in extra income to help keep her family afloat. It was 1920, everyone loved to come and watch Charlie Chaplain movies and Florence was a talented pianist. She had been a good student at the Ursuline Convent School in Westgate -

on - Sea, the nuns had taught her well and she was an accomplished musician.

In 1905 Florence had been sent to the newly opened boarding school by the sea because her father worked for the diplomatic service. Her parents were posted away in the colonies and it was customary to leave children behind in the care of a good school. Gregory was the convent's gardener and they fell in love during her last year at school. Her parents were horrified when they heard the news, and bitterly complained that he came from the wrong side of the tracks. They told Florence in no uncertain terms that if she continued with this most unsuitable relationship that they would disown her. Florence decided to follow her heart, but an early marriage and the arrival of three children in quick succession put a stop to all of her dreams of a career in music.

When war was declared in 1914 Gregory had been one of the many Ramsgate lads who signed up with his friends and work colleagues to do his duty. Sadly, like so many other young men, he never returned home. He left behind a young wife, a war widow, and on the practical side of things there were three little mouths to feed, rent to pay and a lot of stressful headaches to deal with.

Florence was very lucky; a good friend stepped in and saved the day. Rose had been a close school friend and confidant for many years. She was plump and jolly. Her parents also served in the diplomatic service but sadly her father perished in the Great War and now Rose was left to care for her ailing and aged mother. Rose was a spinster, who had never stepped out with a young man, and sadly no one had ever asked her. She resigned herself to the fact that now she was twenty-five years old she was probably well and truly "on the shelf."

Rose could see how much Florence and her family was struggling. She had them all on her mind when she was shopping at Bobby and Co in Margate's Cecil Square. With heavy bags weighing her down she had stopped in front of the adjacent Hippodrome Theatre to catch her breath. It was while she was resting that she noticed the small poster advertising a vacant position.

Experienced pianist required to play during the silent pictures. Occasional evening work available to the right person, apply within.

Rose immediately thought that Florence with her musical talent would be perfect for the job. Florence duly applied; she was far more talented than the other candidates and easily caught the management's eye. Rose had saved the day and continued with her support. She would arrive at Florence's Ramsgate home at six o' clock on the evenings when the young mother was required to play at the Hippodrome. She would play with the children, ensure that they were fed and bathed and that everyone was in bed and asleep before Florence arrived home on the 10.30pm train.

The two friends would sit by the fire for an hour and share stories. Florence told Rose all about the evening's performance. They would laugh over the strange characters that sometimes slipped into the theatre. Rose, in turn, would tell Florence about her day. She would moan about her very difficult, wealthy mother and how she longed to have a husband, her own home and a family. She confided in Florence her own lack of self-confidence, her many fears and how hard she had tried to lose her excess pounds without much success. "Florence, I feel tortured inside, it's all so difficult. I put on a smiling face and say everything is fine but actually that's not how I feel deep down." In turn Florence confided how lonely she felt and bitter that her own family had abandoned her when she had chosen to marry Gregory. War had robbed her of her husband, the children had no father figure in their lives and everything was such a huge struggle. "Rose, I'm totally exhausted and jaded, there's no sunshine in our lives, and we need the earth to move under our feet. Something has to change to make our lives better and worth living."

Eventually the earth did move, and it came in the form of William a tall, robust sea captain with a mop of silver grey hair and a bushy beard. William lived in a pleasant home high up on the west cliff of Ramsgate in Nelson Place overlooking the harbour. At fifty years old he was a worldly wise man. He had begun life as a Ramsgate smack boy but sheer hard work, determination and a series of good fortunes helped him to scale the ladder to better things. He had worked on the steam ships, travelling the world to exotic places, and in more latter years he worked for the Belle Steamship Company. This company owned a fleet of seven paddle steamers connecting Margate and Ramsgate with Clacton, Walton, Felixstowe, Lowestoft and Southend.

William had lost two wives over his chequered life. His first wife had died in childbirth; the baby had been lost too. His second wife succumbed to diphtheria in 1910. He was lonely and when he was off duty and home at Nelson Place he would often take the train to Margate and visit the Hippodrome Theatre to watch the silent pictures. In the late spring of 1920 he couldn't help but notice the new pianist. She was slim, attractive and played with confidence and talent. For many months William kept a careful eye on Florence, then one chilly evening in late September he plucked up enough courage and followed her along Margate seafront to the railway station. As they both boarded the train to Ramsgate he introduced himself and struck up a conversation. To Florence he was a father figure, kind and gracious. For a couple of months they rode together after the show and exchanged pleasant conversation.

It was early December when Florence eventually extended to William an invitation to visit her home and an opportunity to meet with her best friend Rose. Florence always perceived William to be a father figure, she felt that she could talk to him and ask him for advice. He was a good listener probably because he had been to similar dark places. He knew sadness, grief, loss and despair, which were common ground for both of them. However, when it came to romance and love Florence felt nothing in her heart. "Fatherly love, definitely yes, but romance no!" She would confide to Rose, "Romance was definitely a no!"

Rose badly wanted to meet this interesting sea captain about whom she had heard so many stories. Somewhere deep in her soul she knew that this was someone special. William was special; he was like a rock, stable and secure, supportive and kind. He was fatherly to Florence's young children when he visited at the weekends and encouraging to Rose who was such a good friend to Florence.

It happened slowly over the following year, Florence began to witness a blossoming love affair between her best friend, Rose, and her attentive Ramsgate sea captain. It reminded her of the bygone days and the pretty young girl at the Ursuline Convent School who had fallen in love with the gardener, her first and only love. In truth she really missed Gregory but dealing with everyday necessities brought little time for reflection. When she did have time Florence only dwelt upon the bitterness and unfairness of it all. She ruminated upon the deep class divisions in society, the parents who had abandoned her and the awful war that robbed her children of a father and took away her lover. No matter how Florence tried she found it impossible to shake off her festering resentment and anger, it was acidic and ate away at her. While Rose seemed to grow in stature and beauty, losing all of her excess fat, Florence looked in the mirror and began to see an aging woman. Hard work and constant anxiety were beginning to leave their mark. Fine wrinkles and dark circles around her eyes began to appear and she developed a nasty itchy red rash on her arms and legs that would ooze yellow pus from time to time.

It was Christmas 1921 when William finally proposed to Rose. It wasn't much of a surprise to Florence; it was obvious that they were made for each other. However, the choice of a ring was a huge surprise and definitely strange, rare and peculiar. When Rose joyfully opened the padded velvet ring case much to her astonishment she was greeted by a turtle! It was fashioned from 18-carat gold, the shell set with a beautiful sea green opal surrounded by pearls and diamonds completing the head and the front feet. William could see that everyone was surprised and a little taken aback by this strange ring, which was so different. In his fatherly voice he told everyone to gather around as he was going to tell a story. With two of Florence's younger children on each knee they all waited with baited breath.

William explained how he had been born in Ramsgate, the seventh child of a poor family and that his wonderful mother had passed away when he was still very young. There were just too many mouths to feed and his father was finding life very difficult. At the age of 12 he was sent to sea as a smack boy. Ramsgate had the largest fishing fleet on the south coast and there was always plenty of work on the luggers. "We boys lived in the smack boy's home above the sailor's church on the quay side when we weren't at sea. It was a very tough life," William lamented. "I was quick to learn and quick to decide that I wanted a better, more comfortable life than the one that was on offer!" As William continued to tell his story of hardship and suffering it was evident that there wasn't much glamour on offer. He learnt to cook, scrub the decks, sail, tie knots, haul in the fish, identify all the different fish the men caught, mend the nets, watch the weather patterns and determine when a storm was coming. Best of all he learnt to navigate by the stars.

Things took on a more favourable turn in 1885 when he was fifteen years old. He had made up his mind to stow away on one of the many paddle steamers that pulled into Ramsgate and brought visitors from London. "I hid away near the paddle wheels. Eventually, under the cover of darkness, when the ship was tied up at Old Swan Pier in London, I crept out. The big city scared me, I had nowhere to go, just the dirty clothes on my back and a few coins in my pocket. I was very hungry and it had begun to rain." The two younger children stared at William wide-eyed and hung onto his every word.

"My mother must have been watching over me that particular night, I am quite sure of that because I believe that she sent me the kindly gentleman. It was strange; he seemed to appear out of nowhere. He had a little dog and he seemed to sense that I was in trouble. We struck up a conversation and he invited me back to his home for supper. He said that his housekeeper would make me something nice. That was the beginning of something special, the miracle in my life. I had never had a special person in my life before that evening, a person who took an interest just in me, I had always had to fend for myself, and there was never anyone else to lean on. I told him my story. His name was Charles and he said that he had shares in clipper and steamship companies, whose ships travelled all over the world to far off places like America. An old aunt also stopped by that evening while we were eating. She was fat and her face was wizened by age. She seemed to like the chocolate cake. At the old aunt's prompting he told me that he knew all the right people and that he would get me a job as an apprentice on one of the big ships. It was my very first step up on the ladder to success and a better life. Charles graciously let me stay at his home for several weeks while arrangements were being made. During that time his housekeeper took me to the barber's shop for a haircut and then onto some fancy London stores. She purchased three very nice outfits, a little leather suitcase to carry them in and a very warm overcoat, cap, scarf, gloves and new boots for me. I felt like a prince!"

Everyone continued to listen to what seemed like a fairy tale. "The housekeeper had a kitchen maid and between them they fed me really well, when I eventually left I had put on several extra pounds in weight, my cheeks were rosy and my heart was brimming with gratitude." William continued to explain how Charles would sit with him in the evening and tell him stories of all the exotic places that he had visited when he had been younger. He told me to watch out for the turtles in the warm waters of the Caribbean. He loved turtles because they carried their home on their back, their safe place. He said that one day I would have my own home and that in my quiet moments to remember him and always to be kind to others in need particularly those who had no home of their own"

William continued to reminisce, "I already had a good sense of the sea and boats. I could sail, tie knots, read the weather and the stars. My three years as a Ramsgate smack boy prepared me well for what was to come. I was a welcome addition to the steamship crew because I already had my sea legs! Over the next ten years I learnt a great deal including improving my reading and writing. I was determined to make the very best of the opportunity that Charles had given me. I sailed around the world on those ships many times but I never forgot his kindness. Ten years later I was back in London and I decided to call on Charles and thank him. I returned to Old Swan Pier and tried to find the street where his home was situated, but it was so very strange no matter how hard I searched I just couldn't locate that address! In frustration I asked several elderly people who said they had lived in the area all of their life. Each one told me that the street and the house that I so fondly recalled did not and had never existed! I eventually went to the steamship company office and enquired about Charles. Once again no one knew of such a man, they checked all their records and couldn't find a company shareholder by the name that I gave them. However, even more strange was the package that they said had arrived for me a few days earlier. The office manager told me that an old well-endowed lady with a wizened face had called and asked that they give this to me and that I would be calling into the office soon. When I opened the package there was a ring case and inside the most beautiful turtle ring and a simple message telling me to make a home and to be happy! It was all so very strange, rare and peculiar."

Florence and Rose exchanged glances as William continued, "It wasn't long after this strange event that I met a lovely young lady called Grace. I eventually asked her to be my wife. I gave her the turtle ring but she and my son died in childbirth. I was so heartbroken; it took me many years to recover. Eventually I met Anna and she too had the ring, we married but sadly there were no children. Diphtheria took her away from me a few years ago. Of course I have acquired a lovely home in Ramsgate but sadly I have no wife or family to complete my happiness. "

Florence looked down at the ring, Rose turned it over and over in her hands, it really was so very strange and extraordinary but quite beautiful. However, this ring had a past and quite a chequered history. William could sense what Rose was thinking. "I loved Grace and Anna, they loved me too and they loved this ring. We had such happy times together. I don't know why their lives were so short and why they were taken away from me. Sometimes it's not for us to reason and ask why, it just is. The truth is I'm very lonely. I suppose folk always say, third time lucky! "

Rose needed a long time to think about things. She didn't say no but neither did she say yes. William waited patiently, the turtle ring waited patiently and Florence waited with baited breath. Eventually Rose had a dream. An old woman appeared to her, roly-poly with a wizened face. In the dream she took Rose by the hands, looked deep into her eyes and said, "The clocks are ticking Rose. You'll make a wonderful mother; don't leave it until it's all too late. He's a good honest man."

Rose took the dream to be an omen. William and Rose were married in St George's Church, Ramsgate in the summer of 1922. Florence's three children were in attendance. The turtle ring brought good fortune to them all. Rose and William were blessed with two beautiful and healthy children and eventually Florence found her own happiness with a Ramsgate man who regularly attended her piano concerts. Her new husband and the love of her good friends eventually lifted her spirits to a level where she could finally let go of the past; accept it for what it was and move on with energy, renewed passion and love for life. Florence began to live again.

Poppy opened her eyes and smiled at the sparkly treasure. It certainly had a story. As she examined the turtle once more with her long delicate fingers she began to reflect upon the importance of home, a secure place, a loving place where one could set down roots. She felt lucky to be in Margate at Lookout Retreat, home with Aunt Flora and the dogs. She felt the loving embrace of the little town of Margate in her heart and the excitement of her new beginnings in Ramsgate at Madame Popoff's new vintage shop.

A few days later when Poppy was back in Margate working at the Madam Popoff Vintage Emporium she shared the story of the turtle ring. Madam and Isadora gathered around as Poppy showed off her sparkly treasure. Madam smiled and simply said, "It belongs to the sea and to the seafaring community. That ring is far too valuable for our vintage shops but it will find a rightful home one-day on the finger of someone who will truly love and cherish it. The good people at S.H. Cuttings, the Margate jewellers, will help us to find that special person and the proceeds will go to the Royal National Life Boat Institution. Poppy also smiled because she knew that Madam was right, she had learnt that there are some things in life that just aren't meant for us and they won't be happy with us. Madam always knew what to do for the best.

That night, lying in bed at Lookout Retreat, Poppy reflected upon the lives of William, Florence and Rose and once again her mind wandered to the writings of Dr. Edward Bach his *Twelve Healers* and *Seven Helpers.* She reflected upon *gentian* for doubt and setbacks and *gorse* for a sense of hopelessness. Florence, William and Rose would surely have benefited from these at some time in their troubled lives. *Olive* for utter exhaustion would probably have helped Florence, after all she was a single mother struggling to nurture her children and finance the family after the loss of her husband. Probably *oak* would have helped too for struggling on without rest. Rose took a long time to make up her mind when William finally proposed; maybe *Cerato* and *Scleranthus*, two flower remedies for helping one decide, may have helped her along. In the end it was Madam Popoff who finally took action, intervened in a dream, and reminded Rose that she really had a very good man and to acknowledge that the clocks on earth were still ticking and not to leave it until it was all too late.

Chapter 6

"Be not forgetful to entertain strangers: for thereby some have entertained angels unawares." *Hebrews 13:2*

Spring had come at long last. The skies were eggshell blue; and front gardens were a rainbow of colours. Poppy enjoyed seeing all the golden daffodils; the brightly coloured crocus and tulip flowers and she loved to smell the pungent hyacinths. She really enjoyed this special time of the year; it was so full of hope and new possibilities. The freshness and warmth of the sun brought a spring to her step and newfound energy. Jack the Lad seemed perkier than usual. He loved the cliff top bike ride to Ramsgate, Ship Shape Café, Winston and the sausages. The Ramsgate shop had been busy despite the fact that it was still low season but today Poppy was on duty at the *Mother Ship* in Old Town Margate. She still enjoyed her regular days back at the Madam Popoff Vintage Emporium in King's Street just a stone's throw from the harbour. After breakfast she returned Jack the Lad to Lookout Retreat and cycled down Fort Hill towards Margate harbour. To her surprise a very large and lovely wicker picnic hamper had been left by the front door step. Poppy was used to black dustbin bags and tatty cardboard boxes. This hamper was rather grand and in excellent condition. She hauled the heavy basket over the threshold, made a hasty cup of coffee and excitedly opened the lid.

Frankly it was all very disappointing. The lovely wicker hamper was stuffed full of old starched tablecloths and napkins of the sort that one used in the seafront hotels. Once upon a time they had been white, crisp and elegant but obvious wear and tear along with age had produced a pile of limp, threadbare and greying linen. "Oh dear these are disappointing!" Poppy whispered under her breath. She was getting ready to find a dustbin bag as they really weren't suitable for resale in the shop and was thinking to herself that at least the nice wicker hamper could be salvaged when she suddenly felt something hard and lumpy at the bottom of the basket. Hurriedly she pulled everything out and there wrapped carefully in a couple of white tablecloths was a treasure.

Poppy set it gently upon her lap and examined it carefully turning it over several times in her hands. It was a beautiful porcelain teapot probably from the Art Deco Period. It was squat and square in shape and decorated with very brightly painted purple, blue and orange crocus flowers. "Oh this is such a lovely teapot!" Exclaimed Poppy, as she gently turned it over and saw the signature, "this is a valuable Claris Cliff teapot, what a treasure!" As she held it close to her heart she drifted off to another time.

It was the early morning in the summer of 1930 when Margate was busy and the tourist season was in full swing. Archie was lingering outside his stone shed at the elegant Walpole Bay Hotel finishing up a cigarette. The cliff top hotel had been built for discerning guests in 1914 and in 1927 there had been additions and renovations. In pride of place was a gold painted Otis trellis gated lift. The hotel porter was so relieved, it was no longer necessary for him to haul heavy luggage upstairs. Archie had been gainfully employed for several years as hotel handyman and known by all as the *go to man* who could fix anything. He was a big burly Scotsman originally from the small western Scottish island of Eigg where his family had been crofters for generations. The First World War took away most of the island's young men and Archie was one of the few who had returned at the end of hostilities. Island life was never the same for Archie after the war; he missed all of the lost lads whom he had grown up with. Eigg was far too solitary, too quiet; there was just too much thinking time. Archie had too much time to dwell on the young lives that had been snatched away as there were so many families grieving and it felt like an ill wind had settled over the shores of Eigg. He knew that he had to get away to preserve his sanity.

He was a resourceful man. From an early age Archie had learnt to fix things such as locks, fences, pipes, roofs but sadly he couldn't fix the sharp pain felt in his chest and heart. It had settled there since losing so many close friends. Help eventually came from an old aunt who lived across the water in Mallaig. She had been down in London visiting her sister and had spotted an advertisement placed in a popular London newspaper.

Seasonal help required at the elegant Walpole Bay Hotel in the holiday town of Margate, and a permanent handyman position is open to the right applicant.

The formalities happened quickly and Archie found himself on the long train journey south, firstly to Fort William, then to London and finally onto Margate. A new chapter in his life was about to unfold; he was no longer a carefree young man. War, the passage of time and the harsh island life of Eigg had weathered him. His face was rugged and a few deep lines were chiselled into his careworn forehead. He no longer walked with a spring in his step. However, Archie settled well into his new job and the management mostly left him alone.

He was given a stone shed at the bottom of the hotel's garden and it became his quiet refuge. The shed was crammed full of tools, nails, doorknobs and locks, tins of paint and bits and pieces from the hotel all calling for his urgent attention. The shed had an old iron stove on which he could make himself a cup of tea and it provided warmth and comfort in the winter months. Archie's shed was the place where he could escape to when sudden waves of anger, grief and depression reared their ugly heads. Little things brought back the memories of fallen comrades who had been cut down in the prime of their youth, *the lost generation.* Archie struggled with bitterness and despair. He often felt that life was a hopeless struggle and there was nothing that could be done to lift his spirits. He was a responsible, diligent man, but really hard on himself, a man of routine. Everything in the shed had its place including his carriage clock. Time was important to Archie, he was never late, nor was he ever early. He was a man who had put his whole world into a box, confined to four safe walls; there was no room for flexibility or change. On the surface he was rock solid just like the little island of Eigg that had supported his family and friends for generations. However, when all things were said and done Archie felt that life had dealt him a bad hand.

Fashionable people frequented the elegant Walpole Bay Hotel. Archie didn't have much to do with the guests, he kept to himself and when he felt the need for company he would take himself off to the donkey stables by St John's Church. It hadn't taken Archie long to befriend the Margate donkey boys and the older men who would also frequent the stables. There was Ted, Sid and Jack, war veterans and donkey boys back in their younger days. They swapped stories and shared a love for animals. Archie had grown up amongst the Highland ponies of the small isles and he was happiest amongst the animals. He was a big burly man with a sensitive, damaged soul.

Finishing up his cigarette outside his shed on that particular early morning in the summer of 1930 changed the course of Archie's life; it was the day when his sails became trimmed for a more favourable wind. Molly was a fragile young thing, her pale face reminded Archie of a porcelain doll. She was barely sixteen years old and had been employed at The Walpole Bay Hotel for over a year. She was taken on as a chambermaid at the beginning of the 1929 season. As a young child she had been very sickly and subsequently missed much of her education. Molly came from a large, particularly poor Margate family and as soon as she could be gainfully employed her father had made enquiries around the town. The Walpole Bay Hotel offered her a position and a small room to share with two other young maids. Molly needed a lot of support: often floundering in her new job and found it difficult to grasp new things. She was so easily distracted and always seemed to be elsewhere. The housekeeper had to remind her many times how to do things and she was always tired. Climbing the stairs was particularly draining, Molly would gaze lovingly at the Otis trellis gated lift but it was reserved exclusively for the guests and the hotel porter.

Molly spent a lot of time *away with the fairies;* in fact she told Archie that on many occasions she could actually see fairies at the bottom of the garden by his shed. Sometimes they were singing and dancing and sometimes they were weeping. Archie shared her fanciful tales with the donkey boys down at the stables and they all had a jolly good laugh at Molly's expense. This particular day Molly came running down the path to the bottom of the garden in floods of tears and waving a brightly coloured teapot. It was a Claris Cliff teapot to be exact. The porcelain artist was becoming very well known in fashionable circles for her bold brightly painted designs. This squat square shaped pot was decorated with bright orange, blue and purple crocus flowers. The hotel had ordered a number of tea sets to be available for room service in some of the grander hotel suites.

Molly had been tidying up in a suite on the first floor and having become distracted by a noisy sea gull outside of the window, clumsily dropped the lid, which was now badly chipped. Between loud sobs Molly whispered, "Archie I will lose my job, look it's badly chipped. I can't go home again there's no room for me and mother has just had another baby." Archie took Molly's hand and brought her inside his cosy shed. He beckoned for her to sit down on the small wooden bench by the door while he carefully examined the damage. After a long silent pause he announced that there was nothing that he couldn't fix. "Give me time Molly, I have special glue and I'll see to it that no one will ever notice what happened today now dry those tears, all will be well."

As Molly rose to leave she turned to Archie to offer words of appreciation and gratitude but other words just spluttered out across the narrow confines of the shed. "Archie you say that you can fix anything, then why can't you fix those dark grey clouds swirling around you? I see all these bright colours and lights around people but Archie your colours are all muddy and grey. What happened to your light?"

As Archie tinkered in his shed and directed more attention to the damaged teapot lid he mulled over Molly's words. He couldn't see colours around people but he sensed what Molly meant. He accepted that no matter how hard he tried he always felt engulfed in a dark mass, that infiltrated the deepest recesses of his mind and nothing that anyone could do or say seemed to put things right. He felt that when his friends from Eigg had left that a large part of himself had left too. He wondered why God had spared his life on those awful battlefields of Flanders. "Why are they gone and I'm still here?" He muttered under his breath as he deftly handled the broken teapot lid and reached for his small brush dipped in cow glue. He began to ponder over his purpose in life.

Archie had never been a man to ask for help but as he held the fragile teapot lid with his large capable hands and thought about Molly for the first time in his life he prayed for guidance. It came a few days later in the form of a roly-poly woman, her face wizened with age appearing at his shed door and carrying a wicker basket full of yellow flowers. He immediately recognized them to be gorse. Heather and gorse grew profusely in his highland home; these bushes were such familiar sights on the islands and moorlands of Scotland. No one ever crossed the threshold of Archie's shed without invitation. The shed was Archie's very own castle but this old woman, uninvited, stepped inside and firmly sat down on the bench by the door. "Put the kettle on Archie, we'll have a cup of tea and a chat." Archie wasn't sure if she was a hotel guest or a gypsy but before he could say anything she started into a very long speech. When all was said and done she had made him privy to the fact that the bright yellow gorse flowers could help lift his spirits open a window to his heart let in the light and leave room for new possibilities in his life. The old woman told him to find some vases and set the cut flowers around his shed where he could breathe in their loving energy and all would be well. Archie turned his back and walked to the back of the shed where he knew a few chipped vases were stored. When he turned again with three vases in his hands the old woman had mysteriously disappeared as suddenly as she had arrived. Her teacup was still half full but the generous slice of chocolate cake that he had offered was gone.

The gorse seemed to have magical qualities. Archie had set two vases of the cut flowers around his shed and another vase on his bed stand in his tiny room in the basement of the hotel. Over the following three nights he experienced vivid dreams of his long lost friends. They were all running over the wild terrain of Eigg playfully chasing the sheep just as they had always done as naughty young boys. They were rolling in the purple heather and visiting the old Eigg shop and doing odd jobs in return for half penny sweets. On the third night the happy band of friends waved, smiled, shouted goodbye and told Archie to go on. They said it wasn't his time yet; he had important work to do. As they faded away he saw the figure of the windswept old roly-poly woman standing amongst the heather high up on the cliffs of Eigg looking out to sea and smiling. As she too began to fade he heard her voice booming in his ears, “Turn the page Archie, let go of the past, move on, be happy. You have a whole world of wonder ahead of you. Your friends will wait for you on the other side but mind the clocks are ticking here on earth; it’s time to make a change.”

His strange dreams helped to bring closure for Archie. The vases filled with gorse faded quickly as Archie’s spirits began to soar. When he handed Molly the mended teapot lid a few days later she exclaimed, “Why Archie, you look so bright today! I can see all the colours of the rainbow around you; did you find a pot of gold?” Archie smiled, “Molly, there’s no gold pot but I did find an old gypsy woman who liked my chocolate cake. In return she left me with some gorse which is better than gold because it has brought me peace and Molly that’s priceless!”

Archie’s new found peace opened him up to many opportunities. He joined the Garlinge Silver Band. It had been founded in 1886 and was originally known as the Garlinge Wesleyan Mission. Archie played the drums; the band brought new friendships and a deeper, renewed focus to his life. On special occasions he would proudly wear his Scottish clan kilt. As time marched on he met Agnes, a delightful Scottish lady who had come to Margate many years ago to find work as a housekeeper after losing her young husband in The Great War. They made a formidable couple; Agnes received a small inheritance when an uncle passed away and they used this to buy their own small guesthouse on Victoria Road near The Royal School for Deaf Children.

As for Molly, she grew in stature and strength. Archie began to take very seriously her special gifts of spiritual insight. He became her greatest fan and mentor. He would scold others who were quick to laugh at her strange notions. Archie became Molly's much-needed father figure of support; he helped to ground the impressionable young girl and to bring more balance into her life. With Archie's loving attention Molly began to fully blossom. Her compassionate nature flourished and with the help and encouragement of both Agnes and Archie she eventually applied to the nursing school at The Royal Sea Bathing Hospital in Margate. By the time that the 1940 evacuation of the troops at Dunkirk took place Molly was an experienced ward sister. Her special ability to see lights around her patients helped her to discern who urgently needed help. Over the years she had developed her gift of healing touch. Molly could touch her patients and direct healing energy into their sickly bodies. Consequently she was able to save the lives of many young men who were lucky enough to be brought into her ward at the hospital. She was a blessing to all who knew her, it was a life well lived.

Poppy opened her eyes and looked lovingly down at the Claris Cliff teapot with the brightly painted crocus flowers. Upon very careful examination she finally saw the fine lines where the broken lid had been glued together by Archie's capable hands. Madam Popoff appeared from behind the large costume mirror at the back of the shop and as she glided past she smiled. "That's a treasure Poppy. We'll reserve it for occasions in the shop when we have our soirees and bring the community together to celebrate something really special. It's far too precious to price and put on the shop floor, that teapot has a story close to my own heart."

In the late afternoon, as Poppy made her way back to Lookout Retreat, she thought about Archie and the pain and grief that he had suffered from losing his friends. She also reflected upon the fragile, sickly Molly who eventually blossomed into a quite remarkable young woman. Poppy's thoughts then drifted to Dr. Edward Bach and his little tattered booklet *The Twelve Healers.* She felt sure that the flower essence *Clematis* would have helped Molly before she had found Archie's support. Molly wasn't grounded and she was always drifting off to other places, she had found it difficult to focus her attention and to be fully present.

When it came to *The Seven Helpers* that Dr. Bach had described Poppy thought *Olive* might have helped Molly. She had been such a sickly girl. She had little energy and was always so tired. *Rock Water* might have helped Archie. He had been so rigid and hard on himself. He had put his life into a box with four strong, albeit inflexible walls. Her mind then turned to the beautiful gorse flowers that the old gypsy lady had brought to the shed that day. *Gorse* proved to be Archie's salvation. Poppy knew that this flower remedy was for a feeling of utter hopelessness as she had come across it earlier when the elegant black umbrella had come into the Ramsgate shop and she had discovered Henry's story. She had also thought about the possibility of *gorse* for Florence and William. Of course *gorse* exactly fitted Archie's state of mind, just like Henry he had been so depressed and couldn't see the point of carrying on, he had felt that nothing more could be done to make life right for him, he had been about to give it all up. Poppy knew the old gypsy woman was Madam Popoff but she also knew that sometimes in life it wasn't for her to ask questions or to seek the answers. Madam continued to be an enigma, exotic and mysterious. One never knew where and when she would appear but it was always to help someone in great need.

Poppy seriously toyed with the idea that she might be an angel but again questioned herself. "Angels are bright, shining, beautiful beings with wings, at least the ones that I've seen in books and paintings. This one is fat and wizened!"

That evening, back at Lookout Retreat, Poppy asked Aunt Flora if she knew The Walpole Bay Hotel. "Heaven's, yes my dear! It was built in 1914 and owned by the Budge family all of its life, passed down through three generations and they never threw anything away! Sadly, it slowly began to degenerate and in 1989 it eventually closed down. Thankfully it was rescued. That hotel has some special guardian angels you know. They appeared in the form of Jane Bishop and her husband. Against all odds the couple have lovingly restored the old hotel building and made it into a successful business. Love, passion and vision have all brought the old hotel back to life again. They began their restoration project in 1995 as a silver wedding present to each other. Jane told me that the owner David Budge, grandson of Louisa who had built the hotel, gave them

Walpole Bay for five years to see if they could make a go of it. Jane and her husband were total strangers but after meeting them David Budge could see that they were brimming with enthusiasm. Against all odds the Bishops built up the trading figures and completed enough restoration work to enable The Walpole Bay Hotel to be morgageable and by 1998 the Bishops finally realized their lifelong dream and purchased it. It's a period hotel full of the ambience of a bygone era; it has an eclectic social history museum and a unique napery art gallery. It attracts visitors from all over the world. Poppy, The Walpole Bay Hotel has become a destination in its own right. How very exciting that you have your very own story about this hotel! Guests are encouraged to decorate the hotel's linen napkins and they have quite a fascinating display on the walls, a few pieces are by well-known people including Tracy Emin. Uncle Bertie and I used to regularly frequent The Walpole Bay Hotel. Bertie was a freemason and they had all the masonic lodge ladies night dinner and dances there. The basement ballroom has an excellent dance floor. Poppy, we should go there soon for afternoon tea. I'll show you around and introduce you to the Bishops."

That night, in bed, Poppy began to reflect upon the whole notion of angels. It dawned upon her that they actually come in all shapes and sizes and deep within the recesses of her own mind she recalled a wall plaque that she had once seen at a Retreat Centre nestled in the mountains of South Carolina.

"Be not forgetful to entertain strangers: for thereby some have entertained angels unawares." Hebrews 13:2

Chapter 7

Poppy was reading a local history book while she and Jack the Lad were visiting Ship Shape Café early one morning. She was extremely surprised to learn that peacocks once frequented Dane Park in Margate. The exotic birds were eventually banished because they made far too much noise and Canadian geese were eventually moved in as a replacement. A few days later a very large cardboard box arrived on the doorstep of the Ramsgate shop. Queenie, an elegant 90-year-old lady had been sorting through her treasures, recently diagnosed with the early signs of dementia, she had decided to put her affairs in order while she still possessed most of her marbles! Queenie had plucked up courage and ventured up into the attic of her beautiful Georgian home in Albion Place, Ramsgate. There were cobwebs and dust everywhere but she was on a mission and determined to see what was up there in the attic and to sort it all out! She rifled through a number of very old wooden chests left by Emily, her own great grandmother, who had first lived in the lovely house in the 1870's. It was situated high up on the east cliff, and looked onto Albion Gardens and then across to Ramsgate's Royal Harbour.

Queenie had never actually met her great grandmother but her mother had told her lots of stories. Apparently Emily had been a society belle but sadly her life had been short lived because she had died in her mid-twenties of diphtheria. Most of the clothes in the chests were moth eaten and couldn't be salvaged but someone had taken better care of the last chest in which everything had been carefully packed in faded tissue paper and little muslin bags filled with pungent moth balls. It had been filled with beautiful dresses, a corset and a large rather elegant fan perfectly rounded and made from clipped peacock feathers. When most of the clothes had been carefully lifted out and put to one side she also discovered a small rectangular sketch of Ramsgate. The sketch depicted Ramsgate as it had been all those years ago when Emily had lived in Albion Place. The sketch was simply signed *Vincent.*

"Oh! Some wonderful treasures have come my way!" Poppy looked through the large cardboard box that Queenie had carefully sorted, donated and left on the doorstep hoping that they may be of some use. She was particularly eager to know the story of the beautiful peacock fan and was also curious to learn more about the simple little sketch and who *Vincent* the artist was. Poppy had to wait patiently until the end of the day because visitors were already waiting outside for her to open up for business. The tiny Ramsgate shop was in a good position near the quayside and Poppy created eye-catching displays in the two large picture windows. She was so good at pulling in the crowds.

At the close of the busy day she was tired although the peacock fan and the small sketch had waited patiently for her attention. Poppy went into the small back room, made a cup of tea and since her energy was flagging she treated herself to a large slice of chocolate cake. Once settled into one of the comfortable armchairs at the rear of the shop and with Jack the Lad snuggled up on his velvet cushion she picked up the beautiful fan and the simple sketch and drifted off to another time.

It was 1876 and Emily was still a society beauty. Her milky white complexion and her mane of striking red hair turned many heads as she made her way through the town. She was a delicate, sweet, gentle soul, always wanting to help and to please others. She loved to dance and in previous years many young men had competed to write their name upon her dance card. Unfortunately Emily had not made a wise choice when it had come to marriage. At the tender age of 18 she had fallen into the arms of David who was a much older man, handsome and very successful in business. David saw Emily as a conquest and yet another acquisition to his growing empire. He had first set eyes upon the lovely Emily in August of 1869 when they had both received invitations to the opening ball of the Granville Hotel built by Edward Pugin. A whirlwind romance followed and they were married before Christmas. Emily had always lived a sheltered life and simply wasn't aware of the backroom wheeling and dealing that took place in towns like Ramsgate up and down the country. In truth David's wealthy empire was built upon dirty money. Once married and under his tight reins it slowly dawned upon Emily that her handsome husband had a nasty, ugly side and when it reared its frightening head she took to her room, locked the door and sobbed. They lived in a very respectable Georgian home in Albion Place overlooking Albion Gardens from where Ramsgate's Royal Harbour could be seen in the distance. On the corner of Albion Place stood Albion House where Princess Victoria had holidayed in 1835 and had subsequently spent several months recovering from typhoid. Emily's room overlooked the pretty gardens and as time moved on she spent more and more time reflecting over her lot. She began to doubt if she could ever be truly happy again. Emily longed to recapture the innocence of her youth but knew that she couldn't turn the clocks back and that her marriage to David had been a very big mistake.

Frederick, her only child, arrived at Christmas 1870. The tiny baby brought renewed joy and Emily, accompanied by a lady companion, got out and about as much as she could. They promenaded with the perambulator along Ramsgate's East Cliff Esplanade. There was a toll gate so that only well to do middle and upper class Victorians could afford to take in the Ramsgate sea air, all dressed up in their finery. David was away on business much of the time and Emily relished these weeks of freedom. It meant that she wasn't watching over her shoulder in fear every time that he passed by.

The spring of 1876 had arrived and Emily held Frederick's hand tightly. He was now five years old and it was his first day at Mr. Stoke's Boarding School for Boys in Royal Road up on the west cliff of Ramsgate. Emily and her son were particularly close. She directed all of her love into their relationship. Frederick filled the large gaping hole that had opened up in her heart. Her heart was weak and sickly because her home, her safe place, actually wasn't safe at all. David would rant and rave, scolding her over the most trivial of things; he was oppressive and left a dark thick cloud of anger and terror in his wake. There was never any physical abuse only mental and emotional. He manipulated and played mind games as well as he played at the poker tables. He cheated and lied and never played straight either at home or inside the shady business circles in which he slithered.

A young Dutch man called Vincent had taken an assistant teaching post at Mr. Stokes School for Boys and it was Vincent who first greeted Emily and Frederick that early spring morning. Emily was immediately attracted to his mop of red hair as something they both shared in common. From that day onwards Emily always accompanied her son to school and met up, albeit briefly, with the kind teacher waiting on the doorstep. Although Mr. Stokes ran a boarding school he had graciously agreed to take Frederick on as a dayboy. The attraction between Vincent and Emily was mutual. The prospect of seeing Vincent for a few minutes every day brought renewed hope and freshness to her extremely miserable life.

Frederick did well at the school and Emily quickly grew in confidence and strength as the few minutes that she spent with Vincent on the doorstep always lifted her spirits. Several weeks later, on her birthday, he presented her with a beautiful fan made from peacock feathers; saying that the striking blue and emerald green feathers matched her eyes perfectly. The peacock fan opened up a whole new world of conversation between the young teacher and his admirer. Emily discovered that he had a passion for beauty, colour and art and that sometimes in his spare time he would sketch. Vincent also confided in Emily that he was often dogged by overwhelming bouts of depression when he just couldn't see the point of going on. He had come to Ramsgate looking for new direction in his life. Vincent explained that he had spent some time in London working for an art dealer and this had given him the opportunity to visit many famous institutions such as The British Museum and the National Gallery. He liked to read and when he was transferred to the Paris office back in 1875 he had become more religious and less enthusiastic about his job in the art dealership world. He had recently been dismissed and here he was working as an unpaid teaching assistant for Mr. Stokes while he sorted himself out.

Emily and Vincent's relationship was sadly short lived because Vincent eventually found a salaried position at a private school run by a vicar in Isleworth near London. The vicar was going to allow him to preach in the school and in the surrounding villages. It was time to say goodbye. Emily and Vincent both knew that he had to spread his wings; he couldn't stay in Ramsgate forever. His parting gift was a simple sketch of the west cliff of Ramsgate. This was the place where they had spent precious moments on the doorstep, it was simply signed *Vincent.* The sketch and the fan were all that Emily had to remember the passionate young man who had briefly lit up her life.

The autumn of 1876 was cold and gloomy and the absence of Vincent brought more sorrow than Emily could bear. She saw little point in continuing to live in the hellhole that her husband had created in Albion Place. She had nowhere to run to. Frederick seemed happy enough at Mr. Stokes School, he was popular amongst his peers, well-liked by his teachers and he was excelling in his lessons. Emily decided that it was time for her to leave. Diphtheria was in the town and her severely depressed state left her open and susceptible to infection. She had no desire to continue, her heart was weak and there was no joy left in her life only fear and misery. Death would serve as her exit card.

Emily's passing was quick. David asked Mr. Stokes if he would take Frederick on as a boarder and it wasn't long at all before he had another beautiful woman on his arm. Emily's lady companion carefully wrapped her friend's beautiful clothes in tissue paper and slipped them into a large oak trunk that she had hauled up into the attic. Before she closed the lid she fingered the beautiful peacock fan and the simple sketch signed *Vincent* and shed a tear. She had been privy to their story. She slipped these two treasures deep inside the trunk where they remained well hidden and away from David's evil eye.

When Poppy opened up her eyes she gently fingered the beautiful peacock feathers and stared wide-eyed at the simple sketch of Ramsgate signed by a man who was not yet famous. She began to reflect yet again upon the passage of time and the very sad life of a young woman who had succumbed to diphtheria and a brilliant young man who was never recognized in his own lifetime for his artistic talent but glorified by the world in death. For the first time Poppy began to give time, thought and speculation as to what really happens when one reaches the other side. She hoped with all of her heart that Emily and Vincent had found each other again and were at peace.

With tears in her eyes she locked up the shop and cycled back to Lookout Retreat with Jack the Lad, her heart was heavy as she reflected upon their young lives. Her mind turned once again to the work of Dr. Bach and Poppy wondered if the flower remedy *gorse* would have helped both of the lovers in their shared moments of despair and sense of hopelessness. *Centaury*, one of *The Twelve Healers* also came to mind for Emily. She had been so sweet, kind, good natured, yet so weak and vulnerable too. "What if she had been stronger? What if she had been able to stand up to that bully of a husband?" Poppy asked Jack the Lad as she made her way along the cliff top path to Margate.

Madam Popoff immediately recognized the simple sketch of Ramsgate drawn at a time when young Vincent had not yet begun to experiment with colour and paints. "This hidden treasure, if sent to a London auction house, will bring a huge boost of revenue into the flourishing artistic community here in Margate. Think what could be done for the town and the local arts community when this goes under the hammer!" Madam was always so kind and generous; she truly wanted to help people and the community. "The woman is a treasure too!" Exclaimed Poppy a few evenings later when she and Aunt Flora were sharing supper and reflecting upon Poppy's latest story. That night as she was falling asleep Poppy wondered yet again if the old roly-poly woman might be an angel.

Chapter 8

"Time is the coin of your life. It is the only coin that you have, and only you can determine how it will be spent. Be careful lest you let other people spend it for you."
Carl Sandburg

It was late August and the days were particularly hot and sultry. The Isle of Thanet Coast was enjoying a heat wave.

Bank Holiday Monday had seen temperatures of 93 degrees recorded at Heathrow and it was the hottest Bank Holiday on record! The papers and the radio talked extensively about forest fires in the Amazon, too much carbon in the atmosphere, global warming and all of the dangers that faced planet earth. Poppy was relieved to have a couple of days off work to enjoy being outdoors and away from the hot and stuffy confines of her Ramsgate shop. She decided to take a long picnic bike ride out into the countryside. She set off very early in the morning with Jack the Lad snuggled into his wicker basket. The two friends enjoyed the narrow winding country back roads out near the lovely quaint villages of Wingham and Wickhambreaux south east of Canterbury. The leafy lanes offered shade, the hedgerows were bursting with ripe blackberries, trees were laden with apples and farmers had the hay already baled and waiting to be brought into the barns. It was an idyllic day. The blue sky, warm sunshine and the chocolate box thatched cottages with roses rambling by the front door steps brought a sense of joy and hope. Eventually, after much pedalling and the sun was becoming much hotter as midday approached Poppy decided to settle under an ancient oak tree laden with acorns. She propped Dora up against a sturdy gatepost and she entered a large cornfield. The oak tree was in the corner near the gate. Poppy opened up her backpack and pulled out a red and white-checkered tablecloth, which she laid out under the tree. Then she set down a flask of tea, egg salad sandwiches, some fruit and a large packet of crisps. Jack the Lad had not been forgotten, a bag of doggie treats appeared alongside a small bowl filled with water. When lunch was over Poppy remembered the beautiful embroidered cravats that she had hurriedly stuffed into her backpack.

They had come into the shop a few days ago alongside a number of old clothes. Poppy had been so busy with the holiday visitors that she hadn't the time to give them the full attention that they really deserved. She knew instinctively that they were special and were calling to her but it had to be the right moment. Being outside in the beautiful idyllic English countryside seemed exactly like the right time. Sitting under the majestic oak tree with a contented little Jack Russell terrier at her feet was the perfect place to examine the beautiful cravats. As Poppy's fingers gently held them close to her heart she was carried back to another time.

It was 1880 and Jesse was seventy years old and for the past 45 years Sir Moses Montefiore had employed him. Sir Moses was a great man known internationally as an influential Jewish philanthropist. He had devoted his time to protecting the interests of Jews worldwide. He had journeyed to Romania, Russia, Palestine, Morocco and Syria on their behalf. His generosity also supported many non-Jewish causes, which made him a significant role model to the virtues of tolerance and humanity. Sir Moses was a pillar of respectable Ramsgate society. Jesse loved his employer almost as much as he loved his work as a gardener and keeper of the Italianate Glasshouse.

Moses Montefiore had bought East Cliff Lodge in Ramsgate in 1831; an early visitor guide to the area had described it as *a beautiful villa in Gothic taste.* Originally a Mr. Boncey of

Margate had built the villa for Benjamin Bond Hopkins, who acquired the land in 1794. The villa had several owners before it fell into the hands of Moses Montefiore. In 1832 Moses had seen the Italianate Glasshouse for sale in an auction catalogue. It originally stood in the grounds of Bretton Hall in Yorkshire. Curved glasshouses were a way of achieving maximum light. It was constructed of cast iron curving ribs and brass alloy bars. The glasshouse was covered with fish scale glass panes, which became smaller towards the top. Having made the successful purchase Moses Montefiore had it dismantled and carefully re-erected in his estate grounds in Ramsgate.

Jesse came into his employment in 1837 just after Moses Montefiore was knighted. He was a young man at the time, twenty-seven years old, he had lived and worked on his family farm near Maidstone in Kent all of his life. He loved the land and everything that nature had to offer, the peace and the time to wonder at the magic of the seasons, the tiny seeds that grew and fed the village. Jesse understood the rhythm of it all, when to plant, when to harvest and when to give his plants some extra loving care. He talked as easily to his plants as to the stars and planets high above and he knew and understood the relationship the two had upon each other.

It was Jesse's mother who had seen the advertisement for a gardener in a Maidstone newspaper. She worried about her seventh son who had lost his young wife a few years back when she died in childbirth along with their firstborn son. Jesse was finding it really difficult to come to terms with his loss. His mother felt that a change of scenery, getting away from the farm and the village might help him to move on. Jesse was reluctant to pursue the idea at first because the farm and village were all that he knew. They were his whole world but the opportunity to work for a great man captured his attention and imagination and eventually he made the decision to apply for the vacant position.

Jesse arrived in Ramsgate and never looked back. He joined a number of other gardeners caring for the beautiful grounds and the Italianate Glasshouse at East Cliff Lodge. He learnt to care for all of the exotic plants in the glasshouse including the grapevine. He would talk to them all and they became his family, the human family that was never to be. Jesse couldn't bring himself to become involved in yet another relationship with a woman, the death of his young wife and child had been far too much to bear in one lifetime. However, he found solace and healing in nature's bounty and the courage and the conviction to make another path for himself. Jesse's path was similar to that of his employer. It was noble. He worked hard and produced things of great beauty. Jesse didn't have a knighthood, nor did he receive great accolades but in the greater scheme of things he was a great man. Jesse was responsible, reliable, strong, tolerant, loving and compassionate.

His mother loved her seventh son and would always visit him twice a year, once on his birthday in late August and once around Christmas. As she became older she spent much of her time in her armchair sitting by the window in summer or by the fire in the winter and sewing. She made lovely things but the loveliest of them all were the cravats that she made for Jesse. They had been very carefully planned and it had been necessary to put aside some of her housekeeping money to purchase the necessary supplies. It took a year of purposeful saving, every week a few coins were dropped into an old teapot that sat on the highest shelf upon the kitchen dresser. Eventually Jesse's mother had enough in her purse to go to the Maidstone market and purchase good quality bleached cotton and a colourful assortment of silk threads. There were nine cravats in total, three different designs; one was to be used for every day out in the gardens, one to be kept for Sunday best and one for very special occasions such as Jesse's birthday. It was the three birthday cravats that had survived the passage of time; they were in almost pristine condition and were the three that had made the journey into Poppy's Ramsgate Vintage Emporium. Each cravat had a different design. One was embroidered with beautiful oak leaves and delicate acorns; hues of green, brown and golden yellow threads had been used as perfect as the leaves and acorns that Poppy, looking up, could see shading her from the strong sun. The second cravat was adorned with luscious magenta and inky blue blackberries, there were brambles and hovering above them all Poppy could see a beautiful Adonis Blue butterfly. The third cravat was her favourite, an old fashioned bee hive in threads of yellow and gold and a swarm of bees, "Oh my!" Exclaimed Poppy as she carefully examined the delicate thread work. They were clearly a testament to Jesse's love and respect for nature, a reminder of his focus in the world, the place where he felt the most comfortable and most at home. They became Jesse's treasures. His mother passed away shortly after finishing the last cravat. They had been made with and from love, her lasting legacy for Jesse. The cravats were as priceless as the most precious gems that Jesse had seen adorning the elegant ladies who occasionally called at East Cliff Lodge and took tea with Sir Moses Montefiore.

Jesse loved the bees; he fully understood the important part that they played in the cycle of nature. An old beekeeper had taught him how to manage the hives at East Cliff Lodge and Jesse eventually became their trusted guardian. As he grew older and the other gardeners who had once been his contemporaries had moved on Jesse also became the trusted guardian of the Italianate Glasshouse. He was stoical and solid just like the oak tree; people came to him for advice. Jesse always seemed to know the right answer to life's problems. His wisdom was almost sage like, it had been gathered over the many years that he had patiently observed nature. Jesse was a watcher; a quiet man who moved silently, he left light footsteps wherever he trod and the world was a better place because of his gentle yet wise presence.

Today, August 31st 1880, was his birthday. Jesse had chosen to wear the cravat with the beautiful green oak leaves that were gently turning gold and the cluster of acorns. He sat down in the Italianate Glasshouse on this hot day and he started to busy himself with the cactus plants. Many of them needed repotting. Charlie, his trusted cocker spaniel lay sleepily at his feet. As Jesse reflected upon his long life he acknowledged that he had been blessed in many ways and he also realized that he had been a blessing to others. He missed his mother and still, after all these years, his young wife. However, more than anything else, he mourned the child that he had never known. Jesse reflected quietly upon his own seed, which had sadly never taken hold and flourished. He carefully surveyed the glasshouse and smiled as he acknowledged and appreciated all the plants that he had grown and nurtured, all flourishing and happy.

He looked at his pocket watch, midday with the sun at its zenith and it was very hot in the glasshouse. He knew that it was time. Jesse had realized that over the past few years he had become increasingly tired. He had never really taken the time to truly rest, take a holiday and a well-earned respite from his everyday duties. He had become conscious that his memory was slipping away; he had to write himself long lists every day so that he wouldn't forget. He looked down at his hands; the finger joints were becoming deformed with arthritis. Their constant wear and tear in the gardens and glasshouse now made his hands painful, and he knew that it wouldn't be too long before he would find his duties in the garden and the glasshouse difficult to perform. His heart ached for his loved ones on the other side. Jesse decided that it was time. He looked around and smiled, nodded at all of his beautiful plants and he lovingly patted his faithful Charlie goodbye. Jesse shut his eyes and slumped back in his chair.

Charlie immediately sensed that something was wrong and he ran off to bring help. By the time others came it was all too late. When Sir Moses Montefiore summoned his doctor Jesse had been dead for some time. A heart attack was suspected. Everyone at East Cliff Lodge knew that they had lost a trusted friend. The elderly Sir Moses, himself in his twilight years, sighed and muttered to himself, "A good man has sailed away, Chiron the ferryman will be waiting to take him to the Elysian Fields."

Poppy opened her eyes; she was thinking of the Biblical verse three score years and ten. Jesse had chosen to leave just as he had chosen all those years ago to leave the family farm and village and forge a new path for himself. As Poppy held the beautiful embroidered cravat with the oak leaves and cluster of acorns she heard a voice that seemed to come from the ancient oak tree that she was sitting under. "Time, Poppy, we only have so long. Heed the time and make the best use of what you have, make it count."

As she cycled home that afternoon Poppy decided to take a detour and passed by the synagogue built by Moses Montefiore. She had looked up his history on her smart phone and discovered that in 1831, when he had bought East Cliff Lodge in Ramsgate, he had declared that he would build a small but handsome synagogue to commemorate his visit to Jerusalem. He wanted to express his gratitude for a safe journey and to celebrate his great and manifold blessings. On acquiring the house in 1831 Montefiore's cousin, David Mocatta, was hired as the architect. The cost was estimated at between fifteen to sixteen hundred pounds and the interior was an extra three to four hundred pounds. The dedication took place on 16th June 1833. The Grade II listed building is a simple one in the late Regency style and the chiming clock is the only example on an English synagogue. When Poppy reached the synagogue she looked up at the chiming clock and saw that it was inscribed with the motto:

"Time flies. Virtue alone remains."

That evening, back in the welcoming confines of Lookout Retreat Poppy and Aunt Flora discussed the Italianate Glasshouse, Jesse, Sir Moses Montefiore and bees. Poppy produced the beautiful cravat embroidered with oak leaves and acorns and shared Jesse's story. She recalled reading somewhere in the past that the mighty oak trees are often the first trees to be struck down in a lightning strike because on the outside they look so strong and healthy but quite often on the inside they have become rotten. Aunt Flora reflected and said, "Poppy, Jesse worked so hard, and just like the mighty oak he was big and strong and reliable but he never took the time to properly rest. Over time he just became worn out. I suppose it's a lesson we all need to heed, life needs to be a fine balance between work, play and rest that's if we are to maintain good health." Poppy sighed and replied, "Maybe the Bach flower remedy made from the oak tree would have helped Jesse to see that particular nugget of wisdom before it was too late. Apparently it's well indicated for people who struggle on regardless of the warning signs that they are damaging their health." Aunt Flora nodded.

For the remainder of the evening they continued their conversation by discussing the fate of the bees prompted by the beautiful cravat with the old-fashioned beehive. There had been much discussion in the news for the past few years over their plight and of the mysterious disease sweeping through Europe and the USA connected with bee colony collapse. Aunt Flora loved her garden at Lookout Retreat and recently she had decided to help the bees out by sowing several areas with wild flowers to attract and provide nectar for them.

"Loss of agricultural land, encroaching urban environments, toxic chemicals used by farmers and gardeners have all played their part and taken their toll on the declining bee population. Some scientific research has shown that the signal from cell phones not only confuses bees but may also lead to their death. Poppy, bees keep plants and crops alive, without bees us humans wouldn't have much to eat! Einstein is supposed to have quoted that if the bees disappear off the face of the earth, man would only have four years left to live!"

Poppy nodded and sighed, "Aunt Flora I've even read that there's a homoeopathic remedy made from the honeybee called *Apis.* It is an acute care remedy for allergies, bites and stings indicated when there is much redness, heat, swelling and restlessness. I've also heard that many people suffering from distressing allergies have experimented and take a daily spoonful of locally produced honey and over time this can sometimes help their symptoms. Then there's bee propolis. I read about this recently. It's commonly called bee glue a resinous mixture that honey bees produce by mixing their saliva and beeswax with exudate gathered from tree buds, sap flows and other botanical sources. It is used to seal unwanted spaces in the hive. Apparently it has a special compound called pinocembrin, a flavonoid that acts as an antifungal. Propolis is often used in wound healing; a study has found that propolis can help people who have traumatic burns heal faster by speeding up new healthy cell growth.

Propolis has also been shown to kill H. pylori, which is implicated in gastric ulcers and colitis; also MRSA, as in the potentially fatal bug. It acts on these pathogens without destroying the good flora in the gut. Aunt Flora we really do have a lot to thank the bees for and it's good to know that there may be things from the natural world that can help combat some of these super bugs that often make the headlines in the newspapers. They seem to be increasing at such an alarming rate."

Aunt Flora smiled as she rose to clear the supper table, "Poppy we must all learn to take better care of our planet. We need to be diligent caretakers and to truly acknowledge that some of our best healers can be found just outside the door in our own gardens." From the large picture window, as the sun was setting, Poppy could see the wild flowers blowing in the wind and the mighty old oak tree away in the distance at the bottom of the garden on the cliff edge. She carefully packed up the beautiful cravats and as she made her way to bed she wondered what Jesse would have made of it all, the toxic chemicals, the cell phones and the declining bee population.

Chapter 9

Poppy liked to visit Botany Bay in Broadstairs with Jack the Lad. It was on her usual bicycle route along the cliffs to Ramsgate, Ship Shape Café, Winston and the sausages. She often took time out in this beautiful bay with its stunning views. Today it was sunny and warm so she parked Dora against an old wall, plucked Jack the Lad from his basket and let him run off down the beach. He relished this special time when Poppy threw his old tennis ball and he ran happily up and down the beach until he was exhausted. Poppy loved the lily-white cliffs, the crash of the waves as they hit the sand and the scenic chalk stacks created by weather and wave erosion at this windswept beauty spot. She had often reflected and questioned why this magical place had been called Botany Bay. Poppy wondered which came first, Botany Bay New South Wales in Australia or Botany Bay in Broadstairs.

In recent weeks she had read online that until 1782 English convicts were transported to America. However, in 1783 the American War of Independence ended and America refused to accept any more convicts so England had to find somewhere else to send them. Transportation to New South Wales was the solution and many of the convict ships had sailed into Ramsgate. The first fleet of 11 ships left Portsmouth in 1787 and arrived at Botany Bay on the 24th January 1788. Between 1788 and 1868 Britain sent around 164,000 convicts across the world.

Ten common crimes entailed the sentence of transportation. These crimes were listed as follows: petty theft, burglary or housebreaking, highway robbery, stealing clothing, stealing animals, military offences, prostitution and crimes of deception. Poppy had also been very intrigued to read that Ramsgate was often the last port of call in Britain before the prison ships loaded with female convicts set sail for New South Wales.

Today, when she eventually arrived at her Ramsgate shop, she found a small neat box on the doorstep waiting for her attention. It was packed full of very old but pretty ladies gloves all in good condition and hidden deep down amongst the gloves was a little Victorian silver pillbox. The lid had been carefully engraved with the image of a butterfly. Poppy was quite taken with the lovely little box. It was still early in the day and she was eager to examine it and know its story before the shop opened up for business. She hastily made a cup of coffee and settled into the comfy armchair at the back of the shop. Jack the Lad was exhausted from his run on the beach at Botany Bay and was grateful for his velvet cushion waiting for him by Poppy's feet. As she fingered the beautiful little box and gazed at the butterfly she was swiftly taken back to another time.

The year was 1860 and Dolly had journeyed to Ramsgate to seek out and personally thank the well-known and highly respected Elizabeth Fry. Betsy Fry was the face of prison reform in England. Dolly had heard that she suffered from ailing health and had settled in Ramsgate to take in the bracing sea air. Dolly had a past; one that caused her much shame. She had made major life decisions out of necessity. These decisions weren't particularly of Dolly's own choosing, and she had always wished that there had been a better way.

Once upon a time Dolly had been a pretty young girl, her good looks turning the heads of many men who passed her by in the street. The bad things began when she was a young girl of thirteen and just blossoming into womanhood. Dolly lived with her large family in the Docklands of London, an area stretching from the City of London along the River Thames to Beckton. Living in this crowded community was hard and rough; walking the streets at night wasn't safe at all. The little house that the family called home was crowded and uncomfortable. Dolly's father and her four older brothers all worked at the docks. They were strong, no nonsense sort of men, coarse and vulgar. Pretty little Dolly was always frightened; she feared her father's bad temper and the constant hounding that her two oldest brothers dished out. The older boys loved to bully her. In truth Dolly was far too delicate and nice for the circumstances in which she lived. She would shake and blush and occasionally wet her bed at night. She often had bad dreams of being pursued by nasty people who were out to get her and she would wake in the middle of the night crying out for help but no one ever came to her rescue.

Much of the time Dolly was quietly angry, angry at the way she was treated at home, angry at the filth and squalor in which she lived and angry at life itself. It was such a struggle and there was the ever-constant fear that something terrible was about to happen. She never dared to express her anger that would be far too dangerous; she already lived in a tinderbox and she was sensible enough to know that it was best to keep some things hidden so Dolly put on a smiling face to the outside world. So life went on until Dolly was thirteen and then the sexual abuse began. Firstly it was Dolly's own father then it was her two older brothers. They would take her down to the docks usually late in the evening and would use one of the warehouses. At first Dolly was terrified and would struggle and scream but after many slaps, kicks and painful bruises she learnt to keep quiet and obliged simply because it was easier and less painful to do so.

By the time that Dolly had reached the age of fifteen she was ready to escape, she was at the end of her tether. Home was not a safe place, her mother had learnt early on in her own life to turn a blind eye. She conveniently failed to notice her daughter's distress, her bruising and her frightened demeanor. Dolly saw that running away was her only hope of survival. Life was brutal. Every night she woke up from the same awful dream with someone lying on top of her, pinning her down. She felt trapped and struggled to find her breath. It was a warm September evening in 1850 when Dolly finally plucked up enough courage to make her move. She hastily packed up a small bag and slipped away into the starlit night. Whatever dreams of safety and security Dolly might have had on that fateful evening were easily broken when reality finally set in. London was a dangerous place for a pretty, fragile, vulnerable young girl who had already been a victim of rape and sexual abuse. She had a handful of coins in her pocket and no safe place to run to. After a few restless days and nights pacing the streets and sleeping in the parks Dolly was hungry, cold and dirty. Life's necessities influenced the worst decision that she had ever made; she fell from the frying pan right into the fire.

Over the past few days of her aimless wanderings Dolly became aware of a young boy following her. He dipped skilfully in and out of the shadows but he was always there, never too far away. He was aged ten or eleven, slightly built, pale and sickly looking. Dolly didn't perceive him to be a threat and eventually she called out to him. After a brief conversation she followed him back to his home. He easily persuaded her that his own mother had noticed that she seemed to be lost and was concerned about her. Apparently his mother had sent him to follow her and to invite Dolly home for dinner.

Dolly was not only fragile and vulnerable she was also naïve. She listened to the silver tongue because she was hungry, cold, tired and dirty and such an offer was very difficult to resist. Images of a hot meal and the possibility of a warm bed were just too good to look the other way. Dolly accompanied the young boy to a part of London that she didn't know. They walked for the best part of five miles; her feet were hot and sore. Eventually they arrived at a large Georgian house situated in a quiet, pleasant tree lined street. It was painted white and looked very neat and respectable. The steps to the front door were scrubbed clean and there were brightly coloured flowers in tubs either side of the red front door. Dolly couldn't believe her luck. The sickly boy rang the brass doorbell then vanished almost as quickly as he had first appeared. Dolly was recovering from his abrupt action when the door opened and a large woman towered above her. She was wearing a very fancy low cut dress and her face was thickly painted with rouge giving her cherry red lips. The woman quickly looked around and beckoned for Dolly to come in.

The first few days were easy. The woman introduced herself as Madam Violettta. She talked with a thick accent. She told

Dolly that she was French. Dolly was well taken care of and given a very small but nice bedroom overlooking the garden at the rear of the house. The bed had clean, crisp white sheets. Madam Violetta encouraged her to take a long bath every day and to wash her blonde hair. She was given a number of very nice new dresses and matching shoes. It was only after several well-cooked and tasty meals were in Dolly's hungry belly that she began to wonder exactly where she was and why she had been invited here. The sickly looking boy had left her on the doorstep but there didn't seem to be any mother figure in the house only Madam Violetta and the cook who also seemed to keep the house clean. Dolly had noticed that a number of men seemed to come and go throughout the day and she couldn't help but notice the money that exchanged hands when they left.

It was easy to fall into prostitution. Dolly needed food, clothes and a place to stay, Madam Violetta and her business partners wanted young, pretty and vulnerable girls. "It's business," announced Madam Violetta one day after Dolly had spent a week at the pleasant Georgian house. "You can either return to the streets of London or you can choose to stay here. If you stay with me you will have a safe place each night to lie down, you will have food on the table and nice clothes to wear. Of course you will be in my employment and as a working girl you'll be expected to please my guests and give them whatever they request. Dolly it's your choice." So out of necessity, Dolly slipped into the world of prostitution.

She resided at the big Georgian house for two years. Dolly was well looked after but in return it was expected that she should work hard to please the visiting clientele. There was a price to pay. Mrs. Brown, the cook and housekeeper, took Dolly under her wing and taught her how to keep out of trouble reminding her often, “An unwanted baby is the last thing that you need Dolly!” Working as a cook in Victorian England Mrs. Brown was surprisingly well educated and knowledgeable. She took the trouble to sit down with Dolly when they both had time and she taught Dolly how to read, write and calculate. “You won’t always have your good looks Dolly, one day you will have to fend for yourself in other ways.” Mrs. Brown could read the newspaper and she would discuss all the latest news with Dolly. She would educate the young girl in so many ways. They discussed the royal family, the politics of the day, what was happening in other countries around the world and how to manage a household. Dolly’s favourite lesson was in the kitchen, and when business was slack Mrs. Brown taught Dolly how to cook. Dolly learnt so many life skills. These were to become a tremendous asset as the storm clouds began to gather and Dolly’s future began to look less secure.

As the two years passed by and Dolly became so much more educated she began to question the job that she had so easily fallen into at the tender age of fifteen. She hated what was expected of her behind closed doors and she hated herself for not running away. She began to feel ugly and unclean and the more that she dwelt upon such things the more that she hated herself. One day she looked down at her delicate pale hands and noticed a few ugly warts had appeared. Mrs. Brown visited the chemist shop and brought back a number of lotions and potions but the more that they used these harsh substances on her delicate hands the more that the warts multiplied and grew. After a few weeks Dolly's hands looked awful and she had to begin to wear lace gloves to cover them up. The clients didn't like the gloves at all and complained to Madam Violetta. Dolly became nervous and highly anxious and Mrs. Brown once again visited the chemist and returned with special pills to calm her down. She gave Dolly a pretty silver pillbox engraved with a butterfly on the lid that had once belonged to her own mother so that Dolly could safely store the little white pills for her jangled nerves.

Within a few weeks it became clear to everyone that Dolly could no longer stay at the big Georgian house she was no longer the pretty little thing that the clients asked for when they came knocking at the door. Madam Violetta arranged for her to be taken to one of the other houses in a much less salubrious part of London. There weren't any pretty young working girls in these establishments. Dolly learnt that Madam Violetta maintained several houses of ill repute. She lived in the grand Georgian house and was away much of the time overseeing her other business interests. She employed a number of burly men at these establishments to mind the women and throw any troublemakers or unruly clients out. Dolly found it extremely difficult to settle into this new life style. Her hands really bothered her and her nerves were worse than ever. As it was things rapidly took a turn for the worse. Dolly had only been resident for a week when the police raided the house. The women were quickly rounded up and taken to the local police station where they were all charged with prostitution. Dolly eventually found herself in a very crowded, uncomfortable prison cell awaiting deportation to Australia. It was one month later when she was taken to the docks and loaded aboard with a number of other prisoners. Conditions in these prison ships were grim, even worse than the prison cells in London. Dolly knew that if she was to survive she had to use her wits. She was luckier than most because her two year stay at the large Georgian house with Mrs. Brown's delicious food and expert care and mentorship meant that physically, despite her ugly warts, Dolly was in fine physical form. She was no longer thin or sickly and was considerably more robust than most of the other women who shared the same confined space in the prison ship's hold. Dolly was educated enough to realize that she could become sick very quickly in the filthy, claustrophobic, confined space that the prisoners were allocated. Prison ships were notorious for outbreaks of cholera, typhoid and dysentery; Dolly knew that many prisoners never survived the three to six month voyages across the world to Australia.

Dolly's nerves were bad. She had used up all the pills in her little silver pillbox, which together with a change of clothes was all that she possessed in the world. Dolly realized that she was back in the same place that she had found herself a few years back when she had taken the bold step to flee the clutches of her abusive father and her two older brothers. However, a voice deep inside Dolly's head whispered, "No, you are not! You are older and much wiser now. You are better educated and you are stronger. You are streetwise.

Dolly you can and you will survive this awful voyage and you will make a better life for yourself in Australia."

The women on that awful prison ship were particularly thankful for a lady called Betsy Fry. She had dedicated her life to improve the welfare of women prisoners on the prison ships. Betsy had compassion and campaigned for women to be transported without shackles. Many called her the *angel of prisons.* Ventilation below decks was poor and the prisoners were only brought up once a day for some fresh air and exercise. Many were seasick.

Dolly's opportunity came two weeks into the voyage. Their ship had sailed into Ramsgate, the last port before leaving British waters, and supplies had been loaded aboard. Unfortunately some of the barrels of beef earmarked for the ship's crew were rotten possibly they had been poisoned. The cooks who had handled the beef became very sick with dysentery like symptoms and several of them died. Dolly caught wind of this dire news from a few of the prison guards. Eventually she plucked up the courage to tell them that she was a cook, actually a very good cook. She explained that she was capable and experienced and had served her apprenticeship under a Mrs. Brown. The guards were amused as they were fully aware that Dolly's crime was prostitution. However, it was quickly realized that hungry sailors needed a decent meal otherwise trouble would break out on board. Dolly was eventually brought up to the galley to see if she was telling the truth about her culinary skills. She surprised everyone and the galley quickly became her refuge and her mode of survival. She was a good cook and spent all four months working hard and helping to cook for the crew. She was allocated better, cleaner accommodation in the crew's family quarters and this is how Dolly survived. At the end of their passage and once the ship was safely moored in Sydney's harbour a miracle happened. Dolly's grateful captain talked at length to the local government officials and she was granted her freedom. Dolly wasn't taken to the penal colony along with the other prisoners who had survived the dreadful voyage being allowed to freely leave the ship with the crew and the other passengers.

Dolly stepped off the ship into a new land eager to begin another chapter in her life. She was nearly eighteen years old and a pretty young woman. Sadly her ugly disfigured hands told a very different story. She knew that life wasn't going to be easy but she had acquired courage, resourcefulness and knew her own mind. Dolly no longer needed little white pills for her nerves. She wouldn't let herself ever again fall into the depths of despair. Despite her disfigurement Dolly wore her scars well and she shone. There was brilliance about her that others quickly recognized and were attracted to. Jack, one of the crewmembers happened to notice the ragged young lady who stood apart from the others on the crowded quayside. His family had also been on board the ship. Jack had been a soldier and had taken on the position of prison guard to earn passage for himself and his family to the new land. Jack knew of Dolly, her cooking skills and her story. He also knew that a pretty young lady on her own would not survive without some extra help and protection. That day he made an impulsive decision, his wife needed extra help with the children, and their new baby was expected soon. Jack approached Dolly and asked if she would join his family for a few months while they settled into their new home. Dolly breathed a deep sigh of relief it was the gift that she had been praying for.

The accommodation wasn't wonderful but she had a roof over her head and there was always food for the table. Within three months of her arrival Dolly had found her feet. One day when she was wandering around the market place looking for bargains to bring home for the table she noticed a little sign in the window of one of the homes near the quayside.

Homoeopathic Doctor readying to relocate to Melbourne needs an assistant. Cooking, housekeeping and light secretarial skills required. Board and payment offered to the right person. Apply within.

Homoeopathy was one of the most preferred methods of treatment in the middle of the nineteenth century. Mr. Thienette de Berigny and Dr. John Hickson brought their skills and knowledge to Melbourne in the early years. Dr. Hickson already had a practice in Melbourne's suburbs in 1850 and other doctors were eager to follow. A wealthy medical colleague and friend of John Hickson wrote the note that Dolly had seen. He was an adventurer and keen to share his skills and medical knowledge in the strange and mysterious land across the world; he was popular and known to everyone as *the good doctor.*

Dolly returned home and gave the employment prospect careful thought; she talked things through with Jack and his wife and eventually she decided to apply. As it happened she was the one and only applicant as few people wanted to make the long journey to Melbourne and fewer still were single and in a position to take up such employment. Dolly certainly met all the requirements but her checkered past hung over her like a dark shadow. Dolly was lucky that her ship's captain was still in the port and both he and Jack were willing to step forward and speak up for Dolly's good cooking skills, her intelligence and her responsible nature.

Melbourne was first settled in 1835 and in 1847 it had been declared a city. *The good doctor* hired a carriage, a team of horses and two experienced drivers to take them both on the very long overland route to Melbourne in Victoria Province. When he had made the voyage to New South Wales over a year ago he had been terribly seasick for months on end and consequently he vowed that he would never step on board a ship again!

Dolly was extremely sad to wave good-bye to Jack and his family but she felt in her heart that starting again in Melbourne was the right thing to do. For the first time in her life she would be able to hold her head up high and be viewed by others as a respectable member of society. Jack said that they would all miss her but his family also felt that she had a whole exciting world ahead of her and this was not an opportunity to be missed.

The overland ride was gruelling but it afforded Dolly the opportunity to really see and appreciate the strange land that fate had brought her to. The unusual wildlife and the beautiful exotic birds and plants fascinated her. She kept a diary that she would eventually treasure for all of her life.

The good doctor was a middle-aged bachelor, kind, well known and loved by all of his family and colleagues. A family inheritance had left him wealthy and in a position to pursue a life of adventure and to indulge his compassionate nature in helping others alleviate their suffering. With the help of his friend, Dr. John Hickson, he had already made arrangements to purchase a large house that had recently been built on the fashionable Collins Street in the heart of the city. This street had first been laid out in the original survey of Melbourne; the original 1837 Hoddle Grid, and soon it became the most admired address in the city. The homes and rooms of medical professionals dominated the top part of Collins and they all had substantial front gardens. The prestigious Melbourne Club, founded in 1838, was also in this area.

It didn't take Dolly too long to settle into her new life and job. She was efficient, as Mrs. Brown had taught her well in her days spent at the big Georgian house. She had learnt how to manage a household but above all else she was a very good cook. Dolly was appreciated and she thrived. She helped *the good doctor* keep his notes in order, kept his consulting rooms clean and neat, welcomed his patients and carefully watched all that he did. Dolly learnt quickly, she asked if she could read some of his precious books at night when her daily duties were complete and in this way she began to learn more about homoeopathic medicine and the remedies that the good doctor administered. He introduced

Dolly to *The Organon of Medicine* written by Dr. Samuel Hahnemann and she learnt that this whole system of medicine stood upon the foundation of *like cures like* and the *law of the minimum dose*. His curious little white pills are often so dilute that none of the original material could be discerned if a chemist were to analyse the substance in question. Dolly found this particularly hard to get her head around. Some of the philosophy was so very difficult to comprehend but in the end she accepted that the proof was always in the pudding. She looked at the little sugar pills, wondered, questioned and then witnessed first-hand all the patients who did so well on *the good doctor's* medicines and she couldn't help but notice how they would return with their friends and neighbours. *The good doctor* told Dolly that no one had been able to prove exactly how homoeopathic remedies work but he taught her to pay attention to the symptoms, listen and look carefully, use all of her senses, learn the remedies and trust her own judgment.

It wasn't too long before a kitchen maid and a housemaid were also employed to assist Dolly with the busy household. There was always a hub of activity. *The good doctor* liked to entertain so Dolly had to oversee extravagant dinner parties and meetings, which many doctors would attend and sometimes they brought their wives. Dolly welcomed them all continuing to watch, listen and learn. In this way she eventually became his right hand woman. Life wasn't always easy as there were so many diseases and those living in poor, overcrowded, squalid conditions, where good food and clean water was lacking, were often sick. Measles, scarlet fever, dysentery, diphtheria, scabies, cholera and typhoid were always a threat but *the good doctor* seemed to have an answer with his little vials of curious white pills with their cork stoppers. He carefully observed his patients and asked many questions.

Dolly had learnt from her own traumatic experiences the important role that emotions play in sickness and subsequent healing. She knew only too well the misery of abuse and neglect, the heat of anger and the coldness of abandonment and destitution. She knew that when one's spirits were low illness would often strike seeming to lurk in dark corners and basements like a thief in the night ready to pounce and cause havoc. She accompanied *the good doctor* into the poorest parts of the city, the dangerous places, where his own colleagues refused to visit. He had the courage to enter these neighbourhoods and help those desperate for assistance. He refused any form of payment from those whom he knew had nothing to give and in this way he was loved and protected. Everyone in Melbourne knew of *the good doctor* and welcomed him into their homes. When he witnessed young children hallucinating and battling a deathly fever he would look into their dilated pupils, feel the radiant heat from their head and calmly say, "Dolly fetch the *Belladonna*." When his patients lay lifeless and blue he would quickly search in his bag for *Carbo - Vegetabilis* and told Dolly that it was the corpse reviver. Cholera and Typhoid claimed many lives in the squalid neighbourhoods but *the good doctor* always knew which remedies to give depending upon his patient's presenting symptoms. He told Dolly that their symptoms were the signposts to selecting the right remedy and to remember that homoeopaths treated the individual and not the disease. When they lay depleted, pale and exhausted from losing too much body fluid he would reach for the *China.*

Dolly often looked at her own hands, still disfigured by warts. However, as the years passed, there were less of them. It seemed that as she grew in confidence and happiness, deeply satisfied in her role as *the good doctor's* right hand woman, they appeared smaller and were less annoying but they were still there, a poignant reminder of her past. The warts made her feel dirty and unclean and on a deeper festering level she was angry. Dolly often dreamed of beautiful lily-white hands and wondered if there was ever going to be a day when she could stop hiding herself under delicate lace gloves. Eventually that day did come. *The good doctor* had been meeting with fellow colleagues and there was excited talk about a remedy called *Staphysagria* made from the beautiful delphinium plant. It seemed to be very useful for those who had been sexually abused and humiliated, suited to mild, nice people who found it difficult to express their anger. "Dolly would you like to try some?" asked the good doctor over dinner one evening. It felt the right thing to do and for Dolly the curious little white pills opened up a whole new world of magic. Her mood changed, the debilitating headaches that often sent her to bed for a day or two ceased and within a few weeks the warts began to disappear. By Christmas they were gone and for the first time in Dolly's life she felt totally free, she felt that her dis-ease had been vanquished and she knew in her heart that all was well and another new chapter in her life was about to begin.

Dolly loved her new life, homoeopathy and all that *the good doctor* did so in 1859 it really wasn't difficult for her to consent to his most unusual request. He asked Dolly to return home to England on his behalf. She had never anticipated that she would ever again step onto British soil. *The good doctor* loved and trusted her and requested that she visit his family home in the north of England to carefully pack up and return with his extensive and precious collection of medical books and homoeopathic remedies. He knew that Dolly wouldn't let him down. He had been deathly sick on his own voyage to the new land and could never again entertain the possibility of ever returning across the sea himself. A return ticket was purchased for Dolly's voyage, arrangements were made for his brother to meet her in London and to accompany Dolly to the family's estate in northern England where she would spend a few weeks packing up his library and arranging transportation to Australia. She was to personally accompany the precious cargo and to oversee its safe passage.

Dolly arranged to board her returning ship in Ramsgate. She wanted to seek out and personally thank Betsy Fry for all the social reform work that she had done on behalf of women prisoners. So this was how Dolly found herself standing on the east cliff of Ramsgate in 1860 looking out over Ramsgate's Royal Harbour. Today she was a formidable lady, only twenty-five years old but she had acquired enough knowledge and experience to cover many lifetimes! Following several avenues of enquiry Dolly was saddened to hear that she was too late for Elizabeth Fry had passed away from poor health earlier in the year. Dolly stayed in an elegant boarding house up on the cliff tops for a couple of weeks waiting for the departure of her ship.

She had written to Mrs. Brown and was hoping to hear from her. Dolly wanted to share stories of her new life and to personally thank her for all the love, support and education that the kind cook and housekeeper had freely given. When all was said and done she knew that it was Mrs. Brown's legacy that had saved her life. She still carried the little silver pillbox with the beautiful butterfly engraved upon the lid and a few pairs of delicate lace gloves. They were a timely reminder of a scared, lonely, abused young girl who had found healing. Just like the butterfly Dolly's life had transformed and as she fingered the little silver pillbox she accepted that in life anything was possible with the help of a special friend, fairy godmother even.

Just before her ship sailed Dolly received a letter from Mrs. Brown's sister. Sadly the good lady had passed away a few years earlier from influenza. Dolly left the boarding house with a heavy heart and in her grief she completely forgot the little silver pillbox and the lace gloves. She had carefully placed them in the drawer of her writing desk in the elegant boarding house overlooking the sea. The lady of the house had found them, sensed that they were special and had packed them away in a large trunk in the attic of her Ramsgate home awaiting instructions from the pretty young guest who had spent a few weeks waiting for her passage to the new land. Dolly never sent instructions. During that long voyage she was kept busy helping the many sick passengers. She used one of *the good doctor's* homoeopathic kits and saved many lives. When Dolly arrived back in Australia she realized that the silver pillbox and her lace gloves were gone. She looked at her beautiful, flawless hands and the homoeopathic kit of little white pills and knew that her future lay in Australia. Dolly accepted that the past was gone and it was time to live each day as a testament to the love of two very special ladies. Dolly carried Mrs. Brown and Betsy Fry in her heart. There really was no need for trinkets and memorabilia.

Homoeopathic medicine flourished in Melbourne. Dolly and *the good doctor* would regularly meet with other homoeopathic physicians at the rooms of Gould and Martin, homoeopathic pharmacists, at number 90 Collins Street. They discussed the possibility of opening a homoeopathic dispensary in Melbourne. On October 30th 1869 they met with a group of influential lay friends of homoeopathy including some of Melbourne's leading businessmen. The meeting decided to open a dispensary, which would utilize homoeopathy to care for the medical needs of the poor people of Melbourne. The group acted promptly and they leased a house at number 153 Collins Street East and advertised in the daily newspapers and posted placards on the suburban railway stations and opened up subscription lots in order to raise funds. On November 22nd 1869 the Melbourne Homoeopathic Dispensary was opened. Doctors were appointed honorary medical officers and a secretary and a treasurer were added. It was open three days a week and by 1875 there were 695 individual patients and 5,672 consultations on record. Dolly and *the good doctor* were kept busy as homoeopathy continued to flourish and a homoeopathic hospital was eventually opened.

They both lived well into ripe old age but they never married. They were good, loving companions, totally happy and dedicated to their work. They left the world a better place because just like Mrs. Brown and Betsy Fry they had lived, shared, cared and loved.

Poppy opened her eyes and lovingly examined the little silver pillbox with the engraved butterfly; she turned it carefully over in her hands. She decided that she would like to discover much more about this system of healing called homoeopathy. Of course she had first heard mention of homoeopathy last year when she had been working at the Madam Popoff Vintage Emporium in Margate. Poppy recalled Clara's story and how homoeopathic *Opium* had brought her out of her fearful, traumatized state following the physical abuse that she had suddenly suffered at the hands of her brutal husband and the subsequent still birth of her child. Then she recalled Sid's story, the battlefields of the First World War, and the homoeopathic dressing stations, she recalled how the *Calendula* solution that had saved his legs from gangrene. Later in the year, when the Ramsgate shop had opened, a silk smoking jacket led Poppy to yet another *Opium* story and how homoeopathic remedies had helped Lady Louise to reclaim her life and escape from the grip of addiction. Poppy reflected back to her recent conversation with Aunt Flora and the plight of the bees prompted by Jesse's story and recalled how she had also recently read about the homoeopathic remedy called *Apis*.

Poppy had a shelf on one of the oak dressers earmarked for the special treasures that crossed over her threshold. This was a shelf reserved for things of unique interest and value. She looked down at her long delicate fingers and thought about her early days in Madam's employment and how she had first learnt that everything has a story to tell. Poppy was so very grateful that she had honed her skills and learnt to discern the stories. The stories were about ownership, they told what it was like to be human, the good, bad and the ugly. She had learnt about the notion of positive and negative energies, and about the gifts that came when tolerance, forgiveness and love steer one's ship. Of course Poppy had to put a price tag on the little silver pillbox but in her heart she knew it was priceless, yet another treasure. In her heart she knew that someone very special would eventually call into her vintage shop and the silver pillbox would find a new home. Poppy knew that the treasure would choose the right person and all would be well. The silver pillbox would embark upon a new adventure of ownership and belonging.

Chapter 10

"To travel is to live."
Hans Christian Anderson

The Isle of Thanet tourist season was gradually beginning to draw to a close. A few coach loads of elderly pensioners were in town but many of the seasonal businesses were readying to shut during the winter months. Custom was particularly slack at this time of the year. Fewer customers meant smaller profit margins and it was costly just to heat and light the tourist establishments during the winter. Madam Popoff hinted that Poppy should close the shop during the winter months and consider taking an extended holiday. The Ramsgate shop was extremely successful; it was situated in a good position near the harbour and had easily attracted flocks of summer visitors. So many young people, conscious of taking better care of the planet, were becoming more and more interested in purchasing second hand, recycled and fashionable vintage clothing. With all the talk of global warming and climate change young people were becoming reluctant to support economies that produced newly made, cheap, disposable clothes. People were beginning to wake up and acknowledge that these cheap clothes simply drain precious resources and add to the carbon footprint. The Ramsgate shop had buzzed all summer long as young people flocked to the Margate and Ramsgate coast on the weekends. Poppy reflected that it had been over a year since she had last taken a well-earned break and holidayed with a friend in the Alps and Italy. “Perhaps Madam is right, it’s probably time for a rest and a change of scenery,” Poppy muttered to herself as she also reminded herself of Jesse’s story and how continued hard work without a rest had taken its toll.

One cold and rainy autumn day in early October, shortly after Madam had first broached the subject, she took Poppy’s delicate hands and declared, “You need time and space to really reflect upon your life and the path that you have chosen to take. If you truly want to help other people you must put your own house in order. Take time out for yourself Poppy, open the dark closets of your mind, pull out the cobwebs, sweep away the gathering dust and let go of all that is keeping you from soaring with the eagles. I have a brother who lives in Bali. Go to Bali Poppy, explore, meditate, and sit at the feet of the wise men and women, return with your angel wings. Remember Poppy, we dress and mend the broken pieces, that’s what we do here at the Madam Popoff Vintage Emporium. Margate and Ramsgate will wait for you; Broadstairs is also on my mind. It’s your time now, spend it wisely, and I urge you to spend it in Bali.”

Well, Madam had spoken! Poppy had seen the urgency in her crystal blue, all seeing eyes and she knew that she had better do some research on this mystical far away island and perhaps seriously consider the possibility of heading out of town soon. A few days later, over dinner one evening, Aunt Flora pulled out a large manila envelope addressed to Poppy and announced, “The postman left it early this morning, it looks important.” Poppy looked it over and as she hastily tore it open a return airline ticket slipped out. Much to their surprise it was Poppy's passage to Bali. A handwritten note also accompanied the ticket and a small photograph of a very strange looking wizened old man:

"Look out for my brother; he will meet you at the airport when you arrive in Bali and be your guide. He will take you to the Spiritual Centre of the island and introduce you to some of the meditation and healing retreats. Remember to look, listen to your heart, open your mind, learn, let go and spread your wings. Come back to us renewed and refreshed Poppy. We have important work to do, come back to us with hands and a heart filled with light."

Poppy looked down at her own delicate hands and suddenly remembered the story of Archie, Molly, the Walpole Bay Hotel and the Claris Cliff teapot. Molly had been able to see the lights around people and had developed hands of light and healing. Looking at her own delicate hands Poppy wondered if she would find the gift of healing touch in faraway Bali. That night while she was lying in bed she began to ponder over all that happened since that fateful day back in the summer of 2017 when she had seen the discreet note in the window of the Madam Popoff Vintage Emporium in King Street, Margate:

"Part time help needed, only special people need apply."

At long last she was actually beginning to feel special; she was learning to love herself and to value her own gifts and talents. Madam had once said to her, "If you don't love yourself how can you possibly reach out to others with love." Poppy had become privy to so many stories and witnessed what it was truly like to be human. She was beginning to understand the nature of sickness; she had begun to share the work of Edward Bach and Samuel Hahnemann and to talk with customers who seemed to want more than just a new purchase. Poppy knew and understood the two fold mission of the Madam Popoff Vintage Emporium:

"To dress and to mend the broken pieces that's what we do here."

Chapter 11

She had just under a month to prepare for her trip to Bali; her flight was scheduled for November 1st, *All Soul's Day.* She was going to be away for five months which seemed like an eternity, and certainly an extremely long time to be away from Margate, her Ramsgate shop, Aunt Flora, Lookout Retreat, Jack the Lad, Sir Humphrey, Winston and the sausages. Mary was very dismayed when she learnt that

Poppy would be away for so long. "What will my Winston do without his buddy?" She asked glaring at Poppy and wiping the tears from her eyes. Poppy discussed the situation with Aunt Flora and after careful thought her elderly aunt came to the rescue and promised that she would personally take Jack the Lad to Ship Shape Café at least three times every week so that he could meet up with his pal.

Poppy had initially spent several days wondering about Madam's brother. She would pull his photograph out of her bag every day and ponder over the strange looking man. One day, on one of their windy cycle rides to Ship Shape Café, she whispered to Jack the Lad, "Will he be like Madam Popoff, equally as strange and exotic? Is he a gypsy or perhaps he's an angel? Maybe he's a time traveller, or is he simply an enigma? " So many questions came to mind. The most pressing one was why Madam intended to send her across the world to such a distant place. "What will I find in Bali?" Poppy mused.

It was a particularly cold day in late October and very near to her departure date; Poppy was readying the Ramsgate shop for winter closure. The previous Sunday a friend had invited her to take a tour of the Ramsgate Tunnels. As she busied herself in the shop she began to reflect upon some of the information that the tunnel guide had shared with them as they had spent an hour walking through the maze of cold damp tunnels.

Apparently, as the Second World War approached, Ramsgate Borough Council had embarked upon ambitious but controversial plans to create a network of deep shelter tunnels linking to the former main line railway tunnel, which would provide shelter for 60,000 people. Despite initial resistance from the government, but constant pressure from the Mayor of Ramsgate, the plan was finally given the go-ahead and construction began in the spring of 1939. HRH the Duke of Kent formally opened the network of shelter tunnels on 1st June 1939. The tunnels stretched for over three miles under the town. They were 6 feet wide, 7 feet high and constructed to a depth of 50-75 feet to provide an adequate degree of protection against random bombing from 500lb. and 1000lb. medium capacity bombs. There were eleven entrances at strategic points providing refuge within five minutes' walk of most areas. The 1,270-yard long former railway tunnel was also linked to The A.R.P. system. The tunnels were equipped with chemical toilets, bunk beds, seating, lighting and a public address system. Poppy had learnt that the County of Kent had long been regarded as *England's Bomb Alley*. Unfortunately Ramsgate was located at the end of this alley. Consequently, the seaside holiday town was very heavily bombed during the war. When enemy aircraft returned from failed missions they dumped their bombs on Ramsgate before returning home. The first of these raids on the unprotected town had taken place on 24th August 1940. Ramsgate received more than 500 bombs when a squadron of German aircraft were approaching Manston. Their leading aircraft was shot down over the harbour and in vengeance they decided to release their bombs on Ramsgate.

Until her recent visit to the war tunnels Poppy had absolutely no idea how badly the seaside town had suffered during the

Second World War. Being born so many years after the war Poppy had never lived through such terrible times. She had these thoughts on her mind when the shop door suddenly flung open. She looked up clearly startled. There had been no customers in the shop all day. The town was quiet, it was late afternoon, beginning to get dark, and it was cold wet and quite windy outside. However, the door had never opened by itself like this before. A rush of icy cold entered the warm confines of her cosy shop. Jack the Lad woke up suddenly disturbed from his slumbers on his little velvet cushion bed at the back of the shop. His ears pricked up, his fur began to stand on edge and he started to growl. Poppy sensed the ill wind, and as she ran to shut the door she noticed a small parcel on the doorstep. She scooped it up and quickly shut the door. Jack the Lad didn't seem happy at all and Poppy wasn't sure if it was because he had been disturbed by the icy wind or whether something more sinister was afoot. She decided to make herself a cup of tea, sit down and examine the small parcel. There had been no visitors that day and she couldn't understand why whoever had dropped it off hadn't come in to say hello. Poppy was used to people bringing things into the shop, a lot of the locals liked to clear out their cupboards and attics and would often step inside as they dropped things off just to have a chat especially at this time of the year. Many of the older town's folk were lonely and just liked an opportunity to stop by and gossip.

Jack the Lad was very unsettled; he paced around the shop growling as Poppy unwrapped the thick brown paper tied with string. Out fell a number of faded women's headscarves. Although these were old they were currently extremely fashionable amongst young trendy girls. They were the type of scarves that women tied around their heads in the 1940's. Poppy suddenly saw a picture of *Rosie the Riveter* in her mind's eye. *Rosie* was the American poster girl of the 1940's; with her biceps flexed she was the iconic female figure who urged women to do their duty for their country and sign up to work in the factories. Poppy recalled how she had seen several similar posters hanging in the Ramsgate war tunnels museum and on display in the gift shop. They were designed to encourage British women to work in the land army, the fire service or the factories. She gently lifted the most colourful scarf, a red and white polka dot pattern, up to her heart and drifted back to another time.

It was the winter of 1940 and the Ramsgate tunnels had become home to a large population of displaced people. Relentless enemy bombing raids had destroyed many residences in the town. Families with nowhere else to go gathered in the quickly established shantytown. It mainly occupied the former Victorian railway tunnel. The shantytown was a vast underground network of cardboard homes, salvaged pots and pans, paraffin stoves and scraps of furniture. Home was cold damp and smelly. Life was hard. Grief, loss and uncertainty tainted the dank air but with the determined *bulldog mentality* life went on. People rolled up their sleeves they donned a cheerful face and made the most of what was in reality an absolutely terrible situation.

Joy was fifty years old; she presided over the shantytown, a matriarch if you will. She liked to wear a fashionable red and white polka dot headscarf. Joy enjoyed sorting things out, she had a big heart and people knew that they could rely on her. She was also a gossip, liking nothing better than to button hole people and keep them talking mainly about the events of August 24th and her own problems and loss. She had a little wire-haired terrier called Horace who followed her every move and bothered everyone with his constant yapping. Joy and Horace were the face of the shantytown, everyone knew them and they were either loved or were to be avoided at all costs. Joy wasn't always the awful gossip. Underneath it all she was sad and very lonely, her constant chatter covered up her multitude of personal problems and traumas. In her rare quiet moments she would reflect upon the irony of her name. In truth she was far from ever feeling joyful.

In fact Joy always felt that life had dealt her a bad hand. She had been born in 1890 in a boarding house up on the west cliff of Ramsgate. She could never recall much from her early childhood years. However, things took a particularly drastic and memorable turn for the worse when her father suddenly walked out when she was six years old. Apparently he ran away to sea, shirking the responsibilities of marriage and fatherhood. She never saw or heard from him again. He left her mother to bring Joy and her younger sister up alone they faced a difficult life of poverty and social stigma.

From a young age Joy had quickly learnt to become street wise. She was clever and resourceful. In 1904, upon the advice of her mother, she entered into service and worked for a pleasant wealthy Ramsgate family who resided in the town. Over the Christmas holiday in 1913 she married Edgar. They had met the previous year at a festive dance in the Royal Victoria Pavilion, built in 1903 by Ramsgate's Royal Harbour. Joy and Edgar made a happy couple and visualized a bright future together. They had dreams and made plans but then the First World War came along and cruelly stole it all away. It seemed like a malevolent ill wind had blown into Joy's life wreaking havoc and leaving many broken pieces in its wake.

Edgar signed up in the autumn of 1914 along with many of the other eager young men from Ramsgate and the neighbouring towns of Margate and Broadstairs. All of them were willing to do their duty for King and country. When a telegram boy appeared on his bicycle one sultry summer's day in 1915 Joy, barely twenty-five years old, had suddenly become a war widow. It took her a very long time to recover from the grief. Initially she was extremely angry, especially angry when she saw all the visitors in the town enjoying a holiday on the beach. There were donkey rides, bathing machines, the Punch and Judy man, dances at the Royal Victoria Pavilion and the local shops were bustling with customers. Joy found it difficult to understand and to come to terms with the situation. Young men, in their prime, barely a few miles across the channel, in some foreign land, were being slaughtered. She would often mutter to herself and ask the same question over and over again, "How can people sit on the beach and enjoy themselves?" There were many things about life that she found it so very difficult to comprehend.

Following Edgar's untimely death Joy returned to live with her mother in her modest terraced home not far from Ramsgate's High Street. They were just beginning to pick up the pieces when the angel of death came knocking on their door yet again. It was 1917, firstly, the family received notification that Joy's brother-in-law had been killed in the trenches then six weeks later her sister committed suicide. Joy received an urgent message from her young nephew, George that he had found his mother lying unresponsive on the bed when he had returned home from school one afternoon. His mother couldn't entertain the thought of a life without her husband and had taken a fatal overdose of pills. Young George went to live with Joy and his grandmother. They were awful times; it took them all a very long time to recover and to struggle on.

Joy did her best to mother young George but sadly it just wasn't enough. The boy was grief stricken having lost his real parents and several years later he succumbed to diphtheria. There were times when Joy felt that she couldn't possibly carry on. There had been so many dark, miserable, grief stricken years but she simply soldiered on because of her mother. Mother and daughter made a good team. They had both weathered adversity, but they loved each other dearly and found the strength to continue because of their companionship and shared story. They were joined at the hip.

The approach of the Second World War was particularly distressing for both women. It brought back bitter memories of the family's earlier loss. There was Joy's husband, her sister, her brother-in-law and her nephew. Sometimes she felt that her family had been cursed with bad luck. The evacuation of Dunkirk in late May and early June of 1940 saw a lot of activity in Ramsgate. The Ramsgate lifeboat was involved and many little ships from the harbour ventured out to bring the boys back home. Joy was one of the many towns' people who helped out as they were brought ashore.

It was at about this time that her mother, now seventy-five years old, began to have bad dreams. Joy didn't know what to make of it all but blamed the war and all the dead and wounded men that had poured into the town from the rescue ships. Everyone was unsettled; the threat of German invasion was constantly on people's minds. Joy's mother had the same dream every night; it was always in the early hours of the morning at around 3 am. She told Joy that her deceased daughter and grandson visited, they would stand at the bottom of her bed patiently waiting and holding a little yellow bird and they would always say the same thing, "It's time." Joy didn't know what to make of it all.

On August 24th she waved goodbye to her mother at the garden gate. Mum had called out, "Bye, bye honey." Joy dropped Horace off with a friend who lived by the station and who liked to walk dogs. She took the train to Canterbury to visit another friend who was very sick and in the hospital. When Joy returned Ramsgate was in chaos. 500 bombs had been dropped on the town in just five minutes. At the time it was referred to as *The Murder Raid* and was the world's worst assault from the air at the time. The raid killed 29 people, destroyed 78 houses and left 300 homes unfit for habitation and a further 700 homes were damaged.

Eventually Joy managed to pick her way through the devastation and rubble but there was nothing left of her home and mother was gone. It was the worst day of her life.

Joy still had Horace; she would grip him tightly and sob. There were enough tears to fill an ocean. Eventually they went to live in the tunnels along with all the other displaced families. It was a terrible time. As the weeks passed by there were no more tears, Joy learnt to put on a smiling face, rolled up her sleeves and got stuck into making a life for herself underground. Christmas was approaching and some families had brought trees into the tunnel, old shiny baubles and tinsel were procured and everyone was trying to make the best of a very bad situation. The air raid sirens went off from time to time and local people would spill into the tunnels for safety.

It was on one such night, when the air raid warning sirens had brought crowds down into the tunnels, that Joy first noticed an old wizened roly-poly lady watching her. She had such a lovely smile; she approached and easily made friends with Horace. He seemed particularly calm in her presence. Eventually she took hold of Joy's hands, looked deep into her eyes and said, "My dear, you have important work to do. The clocks are ticking and it's time to put your talents to good use for the common good." Joy was just about to question the old lady when the all clear siren sounded and the tunnels quickly became a sea of people heading for the entrances and homeward bound. In the milieu the old lady had quietly slipped away. Joy glanced down at her hands. They felt strange, they had a kind of buzzing, tingling feeling and she could have sworn that she saw a halo of white light around them.

That night when Joy eventually settled down to sleep she had a strange dream. The wizened old lady returned and they were sitting together enjoying a cup of tea and a slice of chocolate cake, a rare treat in wartime England. The old lady told her that she needed to use her hands. "Joy, you are so familiar with grief and depression, you've plummeted to the very depths of despair. Now it's time to use your experiences to help others, help them to heal and to move on, help them to pick up all of their broken pieces." Joy nodded she was all too familiar with broken pieces, the devastation left behind when loved ones have suddenly been taken away, the shock and trauma of it all. Joy knew only too well the broken pieces left by the war and the homes destroyed by the bombs. She knew many of the displaced people some of whom had terrible physical injuries and disfigurement. She knew and hated the cold dark subterranean existence that the war had pressed upon a broken town. There were tears and anger, depression and resentment, doubt and the absence of joy. She had often wondered why she was still here. The old woman seemed to read her mind and said, "the clocks are still ticking here on earth, you are still here Joy and you have work to do, healing work. Use your hands, touch people, sit with them in their despair, there's really no need for words, just sit and be there for them. Send them healing energy through your hands; practice and very soon your hands will become hands of light. Remember, where there is a spark of light there can be no room for the darkness." The dream ended and Joy woke up. She looked down at her hands in the inky darkness of the tunnel and they seemed to glow.

The old lady was soon forgotten as Christmas parties were planned in the tunnels and Joy, always accompanied by Horace, continued her daily life. On Christmas Eve she had yet another dream where the wizened old lady appeared. This time she stood under a Christmas tree and beckoned to Joy. She held out a bunch of the most beautiful lily-white flowers that she had ever seen and pressed them into Joy's hands. "*Star of Bethlehem*, my dear, flowers that help with shock, trauma and grief. Breathe in their healing energy, move on Joy and start to do good work. Use your hands and awaken your heart, you can help people. Remember the clocks here on earth are still ticking. Use your hands of light." The old lady disappeared and Joy woke up with a jolt and once again looked down at her hands, which were glowing.

As Christmas day dawned Joy woke up early and took Horace for a long walk through the town. In the past they would have jogged along the sands but during wartime they were prohibited from venturing onto the beaches. Unlike the First World War the local beaches were closed, barbed wire and booby trap bombs littered the sands with the intent to delay an invading army. On her long walk Joy took advantage of plenty of thinking time. She began to think about the strange old woman and all that had happened over the years, particularly her own loss and pain. She remembered the beautiful white bouquet of flowers and once again she looked down at her hands, which really did seem to glow. Since meeting the old woman in the tunnels and the two dreams Joy had begun to feel better in herself. She looked down at Horace, "What if that strange old woman is right? Maybe I should sit with people and hold their hands; perhaps I really do have a gift. There's no harm in giving it all a try."

Christmas Day 1940 marked the day when Joy's life changed for the better. She decided to act for the common good, it was her gift to humanity. At first it was a little embarrassing and difficult for her to keep quiet because she loved to talk but Joy continued to persevere. She would walk the tunnels with Horace and when she sensed someone was suffering she would offer to sit with them, hold their hand and in the peaceful silence she would focus upon sending them healing energy. The more she practiced the better she became for she could feel her hands tingling and sometimes they seemed to glow. Horace would sit patiently at her feet having stopped the constant yapping and he too was silent. It wasn't long before Joy was known as the *angel of the tunnels.* People would send for her when things took a turn for the worse. Birthdays and anniversaries seemed to touch a raw nerve in most people's lives especially when they had lost a loved one. When someone was particularly angry, depressed or grieving tunnel-folk would say, "send for Joy, the angel with the red and white polka dot headscarf." Joy made a difference to many people who were suffering because they could feel her love and compassion and the stream of energy flowing from her hands which always helped to bring peace and calm, making them feel better and giving them the courage to carry on.

In the aftermath of the war Joy settled down with Fred whom she had met in the tunnels in 1942. He had lost his own wife, son and home in one of the air raids. They made a new life together. Life hadn't been easy for both of them but they had learnt to pick up the pieces and put their best foot forward. Horace passed away in 1950; he had loved Joy with all his heart and hadn't been able to let go. When Joy picked up her old headscarf with the red and white polka dots she always felt his ever watchful presence just as he had followed her every footstep in the tunnels and had sat patiently with her when she went about her healing work. His spirit still lingered with the headscarf guarding his mistress.

Poppy opened her eyes and looked lovingly down at the faded headscarf. That was quite a story. Jack the Lad was still pacing and seemed very uneasy. Poppy sensed that he might be feeling the lingering presence of Joy's little wirehaired terrier, Horace. It was quite late and dark outside, time to lock up and return home to Lookout Retreat. Poppy decided to put the special headscarf on the shelf that she had reserved for her treasures, so it joined the little silver pillbox with the engraved butterfly that had once belonged to Mrs. Brown and Dolly. She left the rest of the bundle of scarves on the coffee table by her armchair with the intent to sort and price them the next morning when she returned.

Jack the Lad was still upset when she returned home. At bedtime Poppy decided to carry his basket up to her room and have him sleep near her for company. That night Poppy had a most unusual dream. A lady with a red and white polka dot headscarf appeared in her bedroom at Lookout Retreat, she was very upset. She turned to Poppy with tears in her eyes as she urgently pleaded, “I need your help. Horace is stuck. He belongs in the spirit world with Fred and I and the rest of his family. He’s too afraid to let go, move towards the light and cross over. We have all been waiting for him. Please help to bring him back to us.” Poppy woke up to the sound of Jack the Lad yelping in his sleep and she wondered if he too had experienced the same dream. She lay awake for hours contemplating how she could possibly help the little wirehair terrier to navigate his way back home to his waiting family on the other side.

As the sun came up she pulled herself out of bed, she was tired and on edge. Jack the Lad wasn’t himself and she worried about all the jobs that still needed to be completed in the Ramsgate shop before closing it up and leaving for Bali. Now she had a major concern and absolutely no idea how it could be resolved. Poppy decided that a brisk bike ride to Ship Shape Café and a full English breakfast would help to blow away the cobwebs and possibly bring her some inspiration. It was a cold crisp day but the sun was shining brightly and the sky was a lovely eggshell blue. The trees in George V Park were turning lovely shades of golden yellow, red and russet brown. Mary, Winston and the sausages were waiting for them. Over a strong mug of tea and a plate of scrambled eggs, bacon and sausage Poppy told Mary all that had happened. She shared the story of the polka dot headscarf, the Ramsgate tunnels, Horace, and her dream. Mary was used to hearing all of Poppy’s strange stories but this one particularly caught her attention because it involved a beloved pet dog. Winston and Jack the Lad had finished their sausages and were sitting with ears cocked apparently listening to every word that came out of Poppy's mouth. After some careful thought Mary said, "Poppy why don't you think about giving that little terrier some of the Bach flower remedies, after all you are always talking about them. You once told me that they are helpful for animals. Do you think that they can help people and animals on the other side too?" Poppy had never entertained such a notion however, it definitely sparked her interest. "Mary, how can I possibly give a flower remedy to a little spirit dog?" Mary, deep in thought, looked down at Winston and Jack the Lad and suddenly she knew exactly what needed to be done. "Poppy choose the Bach flowers that you think will be helpful and put a few drops of each one on that red and white polka dot headscarf, the little spirit animal seems to be attached to that headscarf. If you treat the headscarf surely the animal will receive that healing energy too!" It was a strange but brilliant idea. Poppy couldn't find anything better to match Mary's ingenuity and decided that she would give it a try. Over the past few months she had fulfilled her intention to purchase a complete set of the 38 flower remedies; they were stored in the back room of the Ramsgate shop. She decided to go straight there, do some more research and follow Mary's advice.

After opening up the shop and making herself a cup of coffee Poppy sat down in her armchair and carefully studied the Bach flower remedy book that she had purchased along with her set of 38 remedies. As she thumbed through the information she came across *Heather* it was described as one of *the Seven Helpers*. Once again Poppy was reminded that this group of seven remedies had followed *The Twelve Healers.* Apparently *Heather* is useful for those lonely people who talk far too much about their own problems; they tend to be self-absorbed and much too focused upon themselves. Poppy thought that this flower remedy might have been helpful for Joy in the early months when she had been forced to make her home in the tunnels. Joy and Horace just wouldn't be quiet, then the old lady had made an appearance and everything changed for the better. Poppy knew deep in her heart that the old lady was the mysterious, enigmatic Madam Popoff who always seemed to appear when people were in trouble and needed help.

As Poppy read about *Star of Bethlehem* she was reminded of Joy's dream and how the old lady had pressed a bunch of the beautiful white flowers into her hands and told her that the essence of these lovely spring blooms would help with shock, trauma and grief. Poppy recalled how last year, when she had been working in the Margate shop, she had come across the valuable Beatles record and the story of the two deaf friends. She recalled that when young Cookie had died the old woman had appeared at the Margate Cemetery and had pressed the same bunch of flowers into the hands of Jane her grieving friend. Poppy quietly reflected upon the life of Dr. Edward Bach and his flower remedies and she thought that it really was such a shame that more people weren't familiar with these superior healers of mankind. She bent down to pat Jack the Lad and said, "So many people are desperate when they lose a loved one and often they become stuck in their trauma and grief and they just can't move on." As she spoke these words out loud she immediately knew in her heart that *Star of Bethlehem* would be a good remedy for Horace along with *Mimulus* one of *The Twelve Healers* because it's the flower remedy for fear, particularly known fears. She knew that Horace was afraid of letting go of the headscarf and moving towards the light.

Poppy felt sure that these two remedies would help but a nagging voice deep inside seemed to urge her to look further so she decided to continue to read her Bach flower remedy book. Sometime later Poppy came across *Walnut* the Bach remedy for protection and change. This is a remedy to think about when one is contemplating taking the next step. It seemed to be a good remedy to consider when transitions in life are happening such as moving to a new school, going to college, changing jobs, getting married, having a baby, retiring and ultimately letting go and dying. Poppy knew at once that this was the third remedy, the one that she had been searching for to complete her mission to help Horace to let go and to finally move on so that he could join his family on the other side.

Poppy carefully laid the red and white polka dot headscarf on her lap. Jack the Lad came over and placed a paw on her lap. Poppy could see that he seemed to want to be part of the process. Poppy began to talk to the headscarf; at first she felt quite silly and was thankful that no one else was present. She addressed Horace and told him that she was going to give him some flower remedies so that he could move on towards the light and join Joy and Fred on the other side. "Horace, please don't be afraid we are here to help you. I have three Bach remedies that I know will assist you, they'll help you to let go." Poppy picked up the *Star of Bethlehem* and gently put two drops on the headscarf. "Horace this essence is to help with trauma, shock and grief." Then Poppy opened the *Mimulus*, "Horace this remedy is for fear, fear of letting go, and it will help to give you lots of courage so that you can move towards the light." Finally she gently opened up the bottle of *Walnut* and said, "Horace this is to help you to take the next step, it's the flower for change, you don't need to stay here with Joy's scarf anymore, let go and join her on the other side she's waiting for you and she asked that I help you to make this journey."

Poppy sighed with relief having completed this little ceremony. It seemed such an odd thing to do and she really didn't know if it would have any effect but she knew that she had done her best and it had all been accomplished with such loving intention. Hoping for the best she picked up the red and white polka dot headscarf and carefully set it back upon the oak shelf, Poppy's special shelf for her treasures.

With renewed energy she began to complete all the last minute tasks that awaited her attention. She sorted through and priced all the other vintage headscarves and carefully placed them in a drawer in the oak dresser. She tidied up some of the clothing racks, and then ventured into the back room. Poppy washed and dried the dishes, put everything away, cleaned out the small fridge, wiped down the countertops, cleaned the tiny bathroom, swept the floor and emptied all the bins. She checked that all the windows were secured and turned off the lights and storage heaters then flipped the shop sign to CLOSED. She also put a small sign in the window explaining that the shop would reopen for business in the spring and in the meantime customers should address any enquiries to the Madam Popoff Vintage Emporium, King Street, Margate.

Poppy placed her set of Bach flower remedies in her backpack along with the flower remedy book, she felt that they might be helpful in Bali and she knew that she needed to devote more time to their study. It was three o' clock when Poppy and Jack the Lad stepped out into the bright October sunshine. It was still a lovely clear day, cold and crisp but definitely there was still time and daylight left to treat Jack the Lad to a quick run and ball game on the beach before they headed home on the bike to Lookout Retreat. Poppy still needed to pack a suitcase for her big adventure to the other side of the world but she had a couple of days in hand to complete all that was necessary before boarding the train to London and then onto Heathrow Airport.

Poppy and Jack the Lad cast a joyful picture as they ran along the beach at Ramsgate and played with the rubber ball. It was a beautiful afternoon; she looked up at the clear blue sky and felt that the whole world was smiling with them. After a while she sensed others had joined in too and were running alongside. Poppy couldn't see them but she knew they were there. At one point she felt sure that she caught a glimpse of a little wirehaired terrier running with Jack the Lad. As the happy friends drew nearer to the promenade where she had left Dora, her trusty old bicycle, she heard a whisper in her ear, "Thank you for helping Horace. He's with us now and our family is whole again. The spirit world is smiling Poppy and sending you many blessings, continue all your good work. You are a healer Poppy, remember that there's more work to be done but for now do enjoy your rest in Bali." Poppy smiled, it had been a good day and she was so thankful that she had listened to and followed her heart to help others. Her work had entered a new dimension; today she became conscious that she could actually help both people and animals on both sides of the divide. That was special!

Mary, Aunt Flora, Jack the Lad and Winston stood on the platform at Margate station, it was 10am on November 1st, *All Souls Day*, Poppy stood at the train window waving goodbye and blowing kisses. She was heading for London's Heathrow Airport and a whole new adventure across the world. She was sad to be leaving her friends behind but it felt like the right thing to do and she knew that Margate and Ramsgate would wait for her to return next spring. The train ride would give Poppy plenty of time to reflect upon all that happened over the past year and to think about all the special things that had come into the shop and their stories. It was time to rest, recharge, and reflect. It was time to open a new door in her life. "I wonder what I'll find across the threshold." Poppy mused as she slumped back in her seat and shut her eyes.

Acknowledgements

I am most grateful to and want to particularly thank and acknowledge my editor, Frank Skinner. Frank is the father of Elizabeth, my good friend since childhood. He has known me since I was seven years old. Frank was head of the English Department at Hartsdown Secondary School, Margate and has currently enjoyed many years of active retirement.

My dear friend, Marilyn Pafford, and my wonderful aunt, Lillian Hewson, have spent hours hearing me read my initial manuscripts. They encouraged me to complete *Ramsgate Calling.* Thank you both for your time, love, encouragement and support! Over the years my life has been blessed with many wisdom teachers but I would like to offer special thanks to Misha Norland, Jeremy Sherr, Dr. Jacob Mirman, Sujata Owens, Cilla Whatcott, Hanna and Gisela Kroeger, Jeanette Rohrpasser, Sister Rosalind Gefre and Kevin Doheny.

Although this is a work of fiction there are facts and details pertaining to Ramsgate, Margate and the surrounding area, their history and people. I have used local sources, a few books and web sites to help provide me with background information and they are listed below. I have tried to check things carefully but if the reader finds any errors please forgive me!

Spitfire and Hurricane Memorial Museum, The Airfield, Manston Road, Ramsgate Kent, CT12 5DF

Ramsgate Tunnels – www.ramsgatetunnels.org

"Ramsgate Montefiore Heritage – Town Train & Guide." Leaflet researched by Mark Negin with Hazel Fischer and Rachel Fox

"Glasshouse Glory Leaflet, Celebrating Thanet's Heritage." – Janice Dadds

"Around Thanet. Photographic Memories (Francis Frith Collection.)"

"Ramsgate and Thanet Life. In Old Photographs." Compiled by D.R. J. Perkins

www.yoursourcetoday.com - A 100 Years of History in Cliftonville at The Walpole Bay Hotel 20/05/2014

www.Hpathy.org – A History of Homoeopathy in Victoria. By Dr. Manish Bhatia

www.wikipedia.org - for checking facts especially relating to the convict ships transport of prisoners to Australia and the use of opium in Victorian Britain

"The Medical Discoveries of Edward Bach Physician." Nora Weeks

"The Twelve Healers." Edward Bach

www.bachcentre.com

Author's Note

They say that when the student is ready the teacher appears. I always recall the day, many years ago, when I was browsing in a Minnesota bookstore when suddenly a book fell off the shelf and landed on my foot. It was a book about Bach flower remedies. I have always loved gardening and painting flowers. On that day I made an impulsive purchase. This book changed my life. Dr. Edward Bach has become one of my greatest wisdom teachers. I have a lot to thank him for and I feel his presence in my life daily. He has helped to bring grace and balance to my life and I look to his writings for guidance in all of my work. In 2006 I completed my studies as a Registered Bach Practitioner. (Sally Lynn Tamplin.) In many ways *Last Train to Margate* and *Ramsgate Calling* are my attempts to bring the wisdom of Edward Bach to an even wider audience. I do hope that in some small way my books may be life changing for my readers too. If you would like to discover more about the life and work of Edward Bach please take a look at the Bach Centre web site www.bachcentre.com

Several people have asked me if I have some favourite stories from *Ramsgate Calling.* Many years ago I was visiting a friend in Devon, we were browsing in an old bookshop and I came across the ancient leather bound book by Dr. Joseph Laurie, *Homoeopathic Domestic Medicine,* published in 1854. I purchased the old book and I've subsequently spent many fascinating hours poring over its old yellowing pages and always wanting to write a story about it one day. When I began writing *Ramsgate Calling* there was much talk about heroin addiction both in the USA and Britain and prompting me to write Bessie and Lady Louise's story. Dr. Laurie's home management guidance on the evils of opium addiction was the perfect way to introduce my love for homoeopathic medicine and to demonstrate how helpful it was back in Victorian Britain and currently around the world today. Researching all the topics introduced in *Ramsgate Calling* has been so enjoyable and enlightening. I've grown to acknowledge that people living in the past experienced much of what we are dealing with in our current times. The place, date, clothes, living conditions, transportation may be different but people across the world in every generation have all wrestled with emotions. Fear, anger, rage, hate, greed, sadness, grief, loneliness, depression, indecision, love, connection and joy are all part of the human condition. They colour our lives for better or worse, they determine our health, our vitality and how we are remembered when we have eventually moved on.

Joy of the tunnels has also struck a chord in my heart. Joy's story was born after my husband and I took a tour of the Ramsgate tunnels back in the late summer of 2019. I had no idea how heavily bombed Ramsgate was during the Second World War and how much the townsfolk had suffered. Earlier that summer I had been drawn to visit Findhorn Spiritual Community in Scotland and participated in a seven-day workshop learning the art of hands on healing. My experience in Findhorn helped me to introduce the concept of this amazing healing modality. Working as a healer for many years now I have come to accept that there are many paths that one can take to recover or discover wellness. I feel blessed and grateful that I've had the opportunity to study with so many wisdom teachers. I've learnt the art of flexibility and realize that nothing is impossible. At the end of the tunnel tour we visited the small museum and there was my name engraved upon a St George's School Honour Roll. Somehow a number of the old school boards had ended up in the tunnel museum so part of me is there in that special place!

CPSIA information can be obtained
at www.ICGtesting.com
Printed in the USA
BVHW082237301120
594477BV00009B/1538